# ACKNOWLED

Acknowledgements are part of a book—similar to the one you now hold—wherein the author(s) dole(s) out appreciation for those who helped in the creation and ultimate publication of the volume. Interestingly, and coincidentally, the Acknowledgments page of a book invariably falls either at the volume's immediate beginning or terminal pages, as evidenced in the following example: it must be noted that the compilers of the current volume are grateful to the editors of the journals and magazines below where many of the entries in this book were first published, sometimes in different form:

*Action, Yes*; *Abjective*; *Everyday Genius*, *Hobart*; *Jellyroll Magazine*; *JMWW*; *Keyhole*; *Mad Hatters' Review*; *nth position*; *OCHO*; *Opium Magazine*; *PANK*; *Robot Melon*; *ServingHouse*; *Smokelong Quarterly*; *The 2ndHand*; and on Featherproof Books' TripleQuick Fiction iPhone App.

Thanks to Kevin Sampsell for making this book possible, and to his Future Tense crew: Christina Brauner, Bryan Coffelt, and Brian David Smith.

Thanks to my family: the Iredells and the Babcocks.

Thanks to Christopher Bundy, Mike Dockins, and Man Martin for reading drafts of this book, and to Blake Butler and Spencer, for inadvertently inspiring parts of it.

Of course: Sarah Babcock.

## ACTION FILM, THE

In the action film the hero must have an alliterative name, because it's catchy and everyone remembers it, and it speaks to how badass the hero is. Think B.A. Baracus, think Jesse James. In fact, the action hero's name is James James. When a sultry brunette says, *Hey, who are you?* our hero says, "The name is James. James James." In the action novel there are exactly forty-three explosions. It's hard to describe the explosions, except to say, "The car tumbled down the mountainside, and exploded"; or, "James James was thrown to the ground by the tremendous explosion." That's why this novel will be made into an action film. Then you can actually see the explosions. The female lead looks like a really hot actress. She's hot. She's played by a really hot actress. Back to explosions: James James and his hot actress love interest always jump to safety, even if the tremendously huge explosion tosses them like rag dolls to the ground. Try to get a rag doll into the action film—or the novel. Maybe there's a little girl in there somewhere, James James's estranged daughter from a marriage he lost due to amnesia caused by being thrown against a steel pipe by one grandiose explosion. Worry not about the rag doll; that's why movies have the props department. When these explosions go off, so close that their shock waves toss James James and his incredibly hot love interest to the ground, the heat from the explosion would burn the hair off their legs. The hot actress, though, she doesn't have any hair on her legs, because any girl like that always has her legs waxed. And it would only happen to James

James if he were wearing shorts, but James James only wears shorts in the film's earliest scenes, during a period of relative peace, where he basks upon a white sand shore. Other than that he's always wearing jeans, or cargo pants. He wears the cargo pants because that's where he stores all his explosive devices. It's important to note that James James is a karate expert.

## AFTER DETOX

This is the man who gets a job at a place like Performance Exhaust, after he tells the owner—a skinny Vietnamese named Wang—that he's worked imports all his life, his father a Volkswagen man, his grandfather Mercedes. Wang asks him to look at the automatic transmission on a '94 Sentra. The man laughs, and—no surprise here—Wang hires him.

The schedule is a day shift: eight AM to five PM. At first everything goes according to plan. Our man stumbles in mornings and breathes open the garage doors. His own breath escapes like the fog that sits over the tiny valley where the shop has been planted. Our man goes to work, a car at a time, overhauling engines, transmission rebuilds. Wang wanders in around ten, a Kool dangling from the corner of his mouth, his cellphone hooked onto his belt and constantly beeping that annoying Nextel beep. Wang gets his hands under an open hood and removes a hose. The shop stays open till nine PM and Wang does all the work after our boy leaves at five.

One day, Wang's Nextel goes off and he starts jabbering in his Viet-lingo, then he laughs and jigs around some more in that fucked talk. He lights a fresh Kool. Our man who is fresh out of detox is replacing a blown head gasket on a '64 Lincoln, a beauty, suicide doors and everything. Wang steps away, ching-chonging as he goes. Our man keeps at the Lincoln, but does not finish, as a middle-aged couple's Ford jalopies into the lot, spewing steam and smoke like a dragon. Wang never returns. At five our hero closes the shop doors and goes home.

Next morning, Wang waits for detox-man in the office. The man has never seen Wang there this early. "You lazy American," Wang says. "I leave shop, and you close up, now customer angry." He points at the unfinished Lincoln. Detox-man says that he worked from eight to five, that that was his shift. Wang says he'll pay overtime.

Wang stops coming to the shop in the mornings. Every other day he wanders in around lunchtime, scans the lot of vehicles waiting to be repaired. "Hey lazy white," Wang says. "You work faster, I pay." Then he disappears again, kissing his Nextel.

At lunch, detox-man walks across the street to the sports bar. At first he orders chicken wings and Cokes. Then he replaces the Coke with Budweiser. Then he replaces the chicken wings with Makers Mark.

After lunch, Wang's smoking a Kool in the middle of the car-littered lot. He stamps his tiny oriental foot. When detox-man says he needs help to get everything done on time Wang's eyes grow into tea saucers and his mouth into a donut hole. "Oh, you drunk! You drunk! I smell the booze!"

Wang goes to the office to write up detox-man's last check. Our hero grabs the keys to the Lincoln, which he's now finished and has stashed around the side of the shop. Wang hands over detox-man's check. "You very bad, drunk lazy American," Wang says. Detox-man says thanks, thanks for the job. Wang waves him off like he might wave at mosquitoes. The smoke from his Kool scatters into tiny thunderstorms.

When detox-man drives away, the windows down, the radio playing on the classic rock station (The Eagles), he thinks about moving out of town. He thinks he should go to his room and get his clothes and just drive off. Then, on the freeway on-ramp, he thinks: screw the clothes.

## AMERICANS

If you visit the United States of America, you're greeted by a Haitian, your passport's examined by a Jamaican, your baggage tossed from an aluminum belly by Mexicans. No one ever says that they're American. Ask any of them and they're Irish or Inuit or Ivory Coastian. Almost all of them are Puerto Ricans. Because of this global attitude, Americans think they own everything, especially America, and by that they mean Earth. Americans will tell you that your country has terrible Mexican food. They especially dislike Mexico's Mexican food. Americans reek of petroleum and dream of opening McDonalds on distant planets, which is why all American astronomers are in pursuit of extra solar habitats. Instead of palms and fingers, Americans shake with a hamburger patty and frankfurters. And even the frankfurters—they'll tell you—are better than Frankfurtian frankfurters. The problem with Americans is their annoying politeness: they say, *have some cholesterol, does your daughter speak American?* Your daughter does not. Yet fret not: the American doesn't care. If you do not understand American now, you soon will.

## ARMLESS WONDER

For the woman with no arms, life is a constant dexterity demonstration. Her feet snip scissors through a sheet of cardstock, rectangling out a plane. Her feet ink her signature, lilting in whorls, smooth, seamless as her face. She is Venus—not the goddess, but the planet—a star so bright it blinds, a star with phases: whole, waxing, waning, gone. Her feet caress her husband's skin. Her toes stream his tears, which stream his cheeks when onlookers look on. "It's okay," she whispers. To the starers her feet strike a match and spark her cigarette, tipping the end to the ashtray, butt gripped between big toe and the next little piggy. Her father had called her toes that, piggies, and she laughed and rolled helpless when he pinched a piggy in those wondrous digits about which she knew nothing: fingers. Father sang: "This little piggy went to market, this little piggy stayed home. . ."

## ASSHOLE

This variety of human can be seen in urban areas across planet Earth. He struts down the street, which is more like an avenue, it is so wide. Skyscrapers scrape the edge of the sky—should we consider "edge" as "troposphere"—far above the cars' roofs and above this guy's faux-hawk, both of which are also tropospheric. Below his loafers the sidewalk glitters with spit out wads of chewing gum, many of which spat by our man, for this man decided long ago not to believe in garbage cans. He eschews recycling. All areas where this filth can be found is called "crust." This guy struts and never walks, and while doing so he reads and sends text messages and emails from his smart phone and so never walks in a straight line. It's insufferable to find oneself attempting to pass this man for his weaving. He has a girlfriend, and, at one time previously, had a boyfriend. The boyfriend this guy left, feeling—like one does about quitting in the middle of high school baseball tryouts—that it just wasn't *his* thing, not his "calling". This man, the one we're talking about, is an asshole.

## AUTOFELLATE

This is the act of performing fellatio on oneself, a feat performed at a bar by an alternative circus performer. Also, another, a different guy, sticks a light bulb in a woman's vagina, a woman who has the wires connected to a car battery stuck between her teeth, and this light lights up. All of this, as previously mentioned, happens in a bar.

In the same bar a clown called Piss Puddles the Clown gargle-sings the chorus to "My Sharona" with his own urine. Afterwards he walks out among the crowd where, while inebriated, men who are nonetheless far from the intellectual capacity of, say, Niels Bohr, all shake Piss Puddles's hands and of course those hands are covered with urine.

In this same bar a guy shoots an apple off a woman's head, but it is obvious that the gun is fake and that, probably, the apple has an M-80 shoved into it, or something. This is the lamest act of the night, other than that everyone, including this little circus, gets pretty ripped. Most will not remember how or when they get home.

In this bar a guy autofellates on a bed of nails. Naturally, this guy's penis is on the large side. You kind of forget about the nails.

Also another—a different—clown, nails his dick to a two-by-four then swings his dick back and forth between his legs, so that his dick stretches and looks kind of like a rubber strap one uses to find a vein, pulled taut.

The girl with the light bulb-in-the-pussy trick also has her pussy lips pierced, and she hooks up a six-pack of Pabst to her pussy and swings it back and forth in the same fashion as the clown with his dick nailed to a board.

Then there's a woman who twirls fire and eats some of it. This is also known as fire manipulation. You can find a list of safety-approved fire performers on the Internet; however, like almost everything ever to be seen, this act is relatively normal and totally lame.

## BEARDED LADY

When menopause paused the flow of estrogen and her ovaries shedding eggs, and her uterus its lining, tiny whiskers popped from her chin. At first she trimmed them with her husband's electric nose hair trimmer while he sheared away at their credit card debt and mortgage by trundling his body off to the insurance firm he'd seat belted himself to, a poem-wielding vice presidentialism. Nights this husband returned home still hungry sometimes, even for her forearms against his own. More often for beef liver, onion, potatoes, mashed. His fork was the fork of a forklift and his face the warehouse into which he drove the loads. After dinner: *Law and Order* reruns. He always guessed the murderer before her and for this, and this alone, she hated him.

## BIG LEGS

Breached out the birth canal massive legs first, legs like gas planets, in leg-shape. Titanic legs, unsinkable, sinking through the air of the hospital into the briny wash. Her body: normal as a body, a baby's body: skin and eyes. A shriek like the song of humpbacks. She grew, her legs expansive, exponential. Her legs were the trunks of redwoods. Her legs became Studebakers. She drove forward into redwoods. Everyone stared. *What's wrong with that woman?* Her legs became their own ecosystem: rains of bleach-blonde peach fuzz, clouds of cotton socks and landslides of darkened sweatpants. Custom shoes size eighteen women's. Her crutch is her body, so normal, skin and eyes.

## BLIND

A woman's hips like an Appalachian crest, her breasts foothills: these among infinite eye-pleasures the blind never witness. Take this blind man: his older brother mouthed out descriptions: a dim wood-paneled stair leading to the ladies' rooms, candle-lit. It's like a mouth, the candles its teeth. The browned gold of whisky drizzled from ivory-stained bottles. Among what his brother would never see: the grunts of ramped hips below him, the brine smell of sweat, the air licked their skin, a cavern where sight should've been. The sound of his brother in the next room, not fucking, but sobbing and talking. Whispers about not taking it anymore, that it's too hard. Our blind man, he thinks his brother must mean him, the sight of him, one hand upon his brother's shoulder, as they shuffle after one another down a sidewalk. That is what he thinks—even, what he sees.

## BLURBS

Blurbs can often be found on a book's back cover and sometimes in the opening interior pages. Blurbs consist of short sentences, sometimes whole paragraphs, devoted to developing the ethos of the volume's author or authors, and/or the contents of the work. Typical to the language of the blurb are the following alphabetized adjectives: acrobatic, adversarial, apparent, artful, astute, awe-inspiring, beautiful, big-hearted, bookish, brilliant, brutal, captivating, careful, cautionary, charming, compelling, curious, daring, deft, dubious, enchanting, endearing, essential, evocative, excellent, fascinating, first-rate, flagrant, faultless, funny, garish, grammar-changing, happy, harrowing, haughty, haunting, honest, humorous, indelible, ineffable, imaginative, impressive, inventive, irreverent, jocular, laudable, laughable, likeable, lively, lovely, lush, marked, masterful, merry, meticulous, mournful, murky, nascent, note-perfect, notorious, obsessive, oppressive, opulent, original, passionate, poignant, precocious, promising, rare, relentless, remarkable, revelatory, rich, riveting, skillful, solid, strange, striking, subtle, surprising, tender, timeless, thoughtful, unforgettable, unpredictable, vibrant, visionary, warm, whimsical, wise, xerotic, youthful, zany. There are many nouns used in the blurb (most notably, "debut", as beginning authors are common users of the blurb), and certain whole phrases (example: "tour-de-force") are quite common. Here follow examples of the quintessential blurb:

"Jamie Iredell can spin around with a disc in his hand and then throw that disc incredible distances. He can also do freakish things with words."

—Michael Kimball, author of *Dear Everybody*

"This is a book you will like if you like other books like this. Look at it, look hard, and decide if this blurb surpasses your own wit and literary acumen. Then purchase the book for the retail price, avoiding sales tax if possible. Or place it gently back where you found it, being careful not to bend the pages or smudge the cover."

—Zach Dodson, a Publisher Who Knows

"Blake Aldridge's 'James Uncovered' is a tour de force of modern christian statuary. In its bright and pulsating curves and shadows the attentive reader's rewarded handsomely. Like a fried egg. Or a chocolate strawberry. Or a cow's head in a bright burning sky. The small galaxy of encounters and flesh (or edicts) that is 'James Uncovered' bristles with fierce intelligence and keen psychological wine-insight. Rumi himself would blush and Plato on his brightest day would kneel down in terror because young Blake's sure touch and disarming potencies are capable of taming the most savage monsters as well as inflaming the most spoiled housepets—and I would know: I am one of them! 'James Uncovered' is more than a must-read it is a life-essential: a beautiful gift for the beginner, a delicious surprise for the expert and a total and ravaging miracle-enlightenment for both and everyone in between."

—Ruaun Klassnik, author of *Holy Land*

"This is the book that you should buy for your stepfather next Christmas, if you want to show the unctous, lecherous asshole exactly how you feel."

—John Dermot Woods, author of *The Complete Colection of People, Places, and Things*

"Blurb (blûrb) noun, hence transitive verb. A brief endorsement or encomium usually on a back cover or book jacket. Coined by F. G. Burgess, presumably as a portmanteau of blurt and burble, or else purely for its onomatopoetic quality. The sound is produced by bringing the lips together for a mildly plosive /b/ followed by a liquid /l/ as the tongue rolls from the back of the upper teeth to the lower lip for a comically fat-sounding /ur/ gargling at the back of the throat before terminating with the voiceless stop of a second /b/. Jamie Iredell's *The Book of Freaks* bears the hallmark of truly great literature: it at once delights while making imitation inconceivable."

—Man Martin, author of *Days of the Endless Corvette*

"Jamie Iredell's *The Book of Freaks* is in alphabetical order. My two-year-old thinks he is the absolute shit."

—Todd Dills, author of *Sons of the Rapture*

"A preternaturally gifted new writer [with] a voice that's street-smart and learned, sassy and philosophical at the same time. He damns progress and upholds the ethics of eternal return. Enchanting . . . a startlingly fresh work, an innocent and humorous story about the strangeness of life. It is about youthful dreams . . . and how some of these dreams were fulfilled, and about what happened to those dreamers after reality and old age arrived. It is also a book about ourselves, those of us who shared and identified with the dreams and glories of our heroes."

—Josh Russell, author of *My Bright Midnight*

"When I was 47 I killed a child with a razor bat and a pocket mirror. I had to beat the shit out of that childbaby face so good if it was going to die and I surely wanted it to, for it wore gold slacks, the best slacks to this day still I've ever seen. The good thing is that after I killed the child I brought it back to life, but then I killed it again for smiling. Point is, I have the gift of reanimation, which I picked up because I sometimes look at books and can imagine how writing a book works. Jamie Iredell likes fucking metaphors, but this blurb isn't a metaphor at all. Anything you read in this hot penis-lifting amalgam of Ire-language is meant in private by Mr. Jamie to stand for something else because he thinks metaphors are really powerful. But me, I really killed a child. This is a confession. The child's name was Spencer and he was clean. Next year when I turn 59 I'm going to unmetaphorically kill your fucking dog because fuck your fucking dog."

—Blake Butler, author of *There Is No Year*

"*The Book of Freaks* was pretty good. I liked how the author used American English in a neat way, and how different things and different ideas appeared on different pages, also how there some sentences were long , others short, and the variety was cool. I also liked how there was some poetic stuff, use of imagery and metaphor, etc. I believe the author used simile very effectively. I could not find an instance of foreshadowing that stood out in particular but this does not mean there was no foreshadowing, only that I did not catch it while reading. Despite the lack of foreshadowing, I think the book was pleasurable to read and also informative and edifying and in general I liked it."

—Christopher Higgs, author of *The Complete Works of Marvin K. Mooney*

"I'm too fucking busy."

—Mrs. Babcock, The Compilers' Wife

Clarifendorfum orgefic nallus! Iredell kraddad undistrom addai, blostrum wives, a cat, orange reduction, plarebic destrata a mystery novel calissandic Future Tense. 10,274 ignan . . . o worg.

—Adam Robinson, author of *Adam Robison and Other Poems*

## BOOBS

Boobs are witnessed upon blazing a cigarette through the morning frost. A dump truck's engine's grumbling echoes in the parking garage. The sea gulls flit about, packs of sea gulls like a curtain of feathers falling over the sun. The neighbor's boobs—which is the neighbor, that is, she is nothing *but* boobs—walk out to the mailbox. The boobs climb the stair to the apartment where the boobs do boob things: eat boob-enlarging formulae, and sleep in bras—a boob bed. There are wishes that those boobs could be other people's boobs, that others are in fact a bra-less set of boobs juggling through the office and burning with glares, a thousand eyes drooping and moistening.

## BOYS

This is the common moniker in English for males in the growth periods from newborn to young man. After this period boys are typically referred to as men. Boys can be characterized by their extreme emotional swings, their propensity to violence, and their desperate attempts for attention. For instance, there was a little boy who dwelt in a housing development called Oak Hills, on a drive also called Oak Hills, and one day he got mad at his mother. This was because his mother had taken his stupid sister's side in that fight in the game of Candyland. The boy decided to run away. Before he ran away he slipped on his Superman Underoos, and stuffed his High Sierra backpack with his Batman Underoos and a pair of socks, and other details that would normally be left out. He came to a spot on the edge of the strawberry fields where he liked to sit with his brother and watch the turkey buzzards circle overhead. So he crawled up the embankment to where they'd rubbed the wild grasses flat with their asses, and he took off his backpack. He stared into the sky, and over across the strawberry fields to Meridian Road, where—in a few years—another boy with whom our protagonist played football, would die in a fiery crash, the bumpers and fenders of his Mustang wrapped around an oak. Over there on Meridian Road the boy could see cars sidling by at safe and reasonable speeds. The boy looked again into the sky and this time a cloud floated past. The cloud was little, and did not look like anything, other than a cloud, but the boy determined to keep watching the cloud in the hope that it might eventually look like his dog. He kept watching the cloud until the cloud was just over Fremont Peak. Then the boy became distracted by Fremont Peak, and the radio tower way up at its peak part, near where the boy and his Tiger Scout troop had camped the summer before. They'd played night tag with flashlights up there on the peak. It was fun. By now the boy was feeling a little hungry. He swept up his backpack again and again looked at the sky. Now the cloud that had looked like a cloud looked just a little bit like an evil face, a face that the boy knew the world needed eradicated. So the boy slung his webs to the oaks around him and he pulled himself into the air. He swung from oak tree to oak tree until he reached a trail. Then he lowered himself to the ground again. There he ran into two vampires who tried to bite him, but he knew they would try to bite him because his intuition told him so. So he told the vampires that they couldn't bite him. The vampires looked at each other and said, "Okay. Do you want to come live with us?" The boy thought for a minute, then he said, "Okay." And he went and lived with the vampires and their families. After a little while, the boy went back home to his family because the vampires only ate blood, so the boy was always hungry. His mother was happy to see him, and she said she would never take his sister's side in Candyland ever again. Later the boy would play football, and this kid he played with would die in a car wreck on Meridian Road. But the boy did not know the other boy that well and when it happened the boy did not cry.

## BRICKS, THE

A graph of mud and straw and calloused hands. Fingers like worms inching through soil and kneading out mortar. He'd cased them. They: these worn-handed workers who walled themselves, by his—the king's—order. He ordered a palace built, and the builders came to blows, which is why the father's eyes have swollen shut, and the oldest son's knuckles are bright plums. The mother and two daughters (their saliva running thread-like from the seams of their mouths and pooling between their legs as tiny lakes, as spools of saliva-thread) stare, their eyes whiter, for their rags have browned as brown as their skin, which is black. Black shadows cast from the walls, which are symbols of their lives and of their class, as the walls shadow them and everyone beyond the walls, and the entire kingdom, even him—the king—who as far as he can tell has been unsuccessful at cutting away his own shadow. His heels have scarred and he's lost every toe, and where the toes once were now skin smooth like a burn victim's skin would shine if there were sunlight. But he stares at his walls, though he himself has not been walled, and he wishes he could hide its shadow, for he forgot in his manic walling to wall himself. Within a wall there are only shadows and so there aren't any shadows at all.

## CHICKEN FRIED STEAK

Chicken fried steak is a common American breakfast and dinner food item that is not chicken, but a cube steak breaded and fried in the style of Southern fried chicken. A man named Jesse once wanted to order one. Jesse tripped down Fourth Street for four blocks before he found a nickel taking up space between the sections of sidewalk. He took the nickel into the Alturas and put it, along with the other two nickels and the dime he already had in his pocket, on the bar. The bartender took them in and returned to Jesse a quarter. At the door sat candy machines and Jesse inserted his quarter and scored about seven Skittles.

There had been a rash of car break-ins. Glass littered the streetsides like millions of diamonds. The air hung cold, the sky white, and a few snowflakes fluttered down. The last of Jesse's Skittles got so cold they hurt his teeth when he crunched into them.

The Alturas was a biker and blues bar. Once Jesse had danced there with an ex who promptly (on the same night) became angered over a drink Jesse bought for his best friend's girl, Mari. His best friend's name was Mario, and Jesse thought that that was proof of a perfect match. Jesse couldn't remember the angry ex's name. Jesse supposed that these facts were grounds for the angry ex not being a girlfriend at all. He considered that perhaps Mario and Mari were not friends, especially since he didn't hang with them anymore, but then he thought that since he remembered their names it was okay. He was about even with Ed's Alley Inn. Ed's was a bar/restaurant. Jesse considered a chicken fried steak. The chicken fried steaks at Ed's were the best he'd ever had. But he'd spent the only quarter he had on Skittles, so a chicken fried steak was off.

Meantime, on the slopes of Mount Rose, a group of snowboarders were cutting through new powder on their way down the mountainside. When boarding in the wilderness, avalanches are notorious for overtaking snowboarders, then they're buried, and only rarely recovered and brought to safety. These guys cruised across the snow whooping and hollering with glee.

## CELEBRITIES

See *Asshole* (pg. 9). Fruit—diced—and nonfat yogurt, pixelate the celebrity's breakfast table. Paparazzi line like army ants fanning out a circumference of rainforest. Coke lines the bathroom countertops. Televisions spit life lies worldwide. When a daughter squeezes through and is christened Mountain, Stream, Native American of the Plains States, Star Lemon, the divorce papers file in—a stack of plant cells. And even the mitochondria of those plant cells have filed microscopic divorce papers, their photosynthetic component partners bleached and thick as cell Constitutions spelling Life, Liberty, We the Cells, Custody. Wrinkles botoxed smooth, a placid sea; the ass lipoed, unchunked. The tabloids scream—literally—"Guess who!?" Mothers lined like already-mentioned army ants at Schnucks across Iowa cry in the land where they let the mothers cry. Their children, fenced into grocery carts, and the frat boys, their polo collars upturned, pick their noses and blink in the blinding white light.

## COLOPHON

This book was set in Caslon, a font designed by William Caslon, the famous English typesetter, designer, and gunsmith. Despite the continued popularity of the use of his font in books, Caslon's original intent was for the design to be used for stamping his prototype of the .357 revolver, which had then never before been seen. Caslon was known to hunt foxes, but his deviations in the deserts of northern Nevada, where he rode upon his knees in the bed of a Toyota pickup nighttimes, spotlighting jackrabbits and blowing them away with his experimental weapon, are only now being revealed. It is said that Caslon lost his favorite powdered wig upon bumping into a then-recent flash flood wash, and the wig went unrecovered, presumably, buried under the desert's drifting soil. The editor of this particular volume was Kevin Sampsell, American author of, most recently, *A Common Pornography* (Harper Perennial, 2010). The cover art is "The Hawain Tryptych", by Hieronymous Bosch. The designer was Mike Dockins, author of *Slouching in the Path of What the Fuck is That?* (Sage Hill Press, 2007), and *Letter to Some Person from Some Place* (???????).

## COLOR BLIND

This is the condition of being incapable of distinguishing colors. There was a man who was color blind. His mother blubbered that the tiny crystals—excavated from the dirt road along the meadow winding river-like beneath Crystal Peak—rubbed upon one's wrists would send one nirvana-bound. This same woman's splash of tie dye in skirts and t-shirts, headbands for the sweat she never sweated, except when the LSD wound its way into her blood and her neck, which she rubbed, seemed to whisper *oh god what a rush, oh god you have to try this*. He knew, in reality, that everyone was different, and that some didn't deserve. Like his mother, who was too stupid. Like the color blind man, who knew he should be locked up. He kept an apartment on Boulevard, in a neighborhood his mother called "colorful". He bought lottery tickets at his building's ground-level convenience store, the Korean owner mouthing *hello mister, you want Lucky Eights again today?* The Easy Shop's windows were barred against the light and color of the Earth. This man, our hero, never won the lottery, and wasn't sure he wanted to.

## COMIC DORK

Sometimes during the comic dork's nightmares—bowie knife-wielding bearded goons hanging over his chest, strapped as he was to the vinyl of the Beetle's interior—he'd realize that he was dreaming. Taken from films and pseudoscientific peyote poppers, he'd imagine himself like Wolverine, the comic book guy. When the claws flicked out, painlessly, from the backs of his downed knuckles, his perpetrator would laugh and drive the knife point into the boy's neck. "What do you think this is," the man reeking of Skoal spit. "This ain't no dream." The boy always woke and lay in bed. After a while he fell back asleep. In the mornings as he brushed his teeth, his mother lay her Dawn-soft hands on his shoulders, and rubbed Vaseline into the split of his lip.

## CONTRARIANS

The Contrarian is from a region where no one agrees with anyone else. You say archipElago, the Contrarian says archipelAgo. Contrarians show up at folks' dinner parties flouting their non-ownership of cable television because this, they know, is contrary. Contrarians tell you things you know cannot be true. The polar ice caps cannot be shrinking that quickly, can they? And what will we do with all these humans, according to the Contrarian's view on the planet-wide overpopulation catastrophe? Contrarians, while entertaining during election periods, are a terrible nuisance at your church's Ballroom Night Fundraiser. They say, *Benny Goodman, hmph!* All anyone can do with a Contrarian is agree with him. This puts Contrarians into exciteable states. Should they continue to be contrary and go against their own opinions? You have thus turned a Contrarian from his own side of his truth, kind of like a Jedi who has ceased believing in the stupid fake benevolence of his order, which could really only happen in a dumb movie because people aren't really that good, no matter what. If you want to make a Contrarian no longer contrary, simply agree with him. This is a logical paradox. We are also confused.

# COPYRIGHT

This important part of a book contains the necessary legal information pertaining to the book's publication, as well as any caveats concerning the material the book covers.

For example the information concerning the present volume is as follows:



Cover design by Bryan Coffelt and Brian David Smith. Photo by Brian David Smith.

Edited by Kevin Sampsell and Christina Brauner.

First Edition



ISBN 10: 1-892061-39-2
ISBN 13: 978-1-892061-39-3

Future Tense Books
P.O. Box 42416
Portland, OR 97242

www.futuretensebooks.com

## COURTSHIP

This is mimicry of all mimicking animal and plant life. This is woman: the reason for cologne and four-by-four pick-ups. The bottle helps, cause of and solution to all human wrinkles. So too the pen. And insomnia. Many have a laundry list—of all things to list. Nearly filling the list are socks. Fifty-two individual white socks. Six of various colors. Next: T-shirts, mostly black. And in the pants' pockets: other lists. They are all for groceries: eggs, bread, aftershave, a trove of fall mums. This is all more mimicry for woman. Also, too much beer.

## DANES

One legend concerning the foundation of the country today known as Denmark concerns a man named Dan. Adolf said, Let's kill the Jutes. Gunvor said, I'm for the destruction of the Romans. Kresten said, Let's hear what Dan the Zeal has to say. We should see what Dan thinks. Dan was all like, let's kill the Romans, and go to In-N-Out Burger. Dan would typically order a 6x6, Animal Style, but after that one asshole ordered the 100x100 now the In-N-Out will only let you go as high as 4x4, so that was what Dan would get if Dan were still alive today. It is inconclusive whether or not Dan's death was directly related to In-N-Out consumption. That has not stopped Signe, who has waged a rather ill-conceived plot of revenge against her uncle Jarl, proprietor of the Solvang, California In-N-Out, where sales have gone tre høj. Solvang, it should be noted, was founded by Danes in search of respite from Midwestern winters, which is fucking weird because they're fucking Danish. Danes sweat in ten Celsius. One noted Solvangian, Søren Andersen, replied, I hate snow, and fish, and Danishes. That's why I live here in Solvang, where one's served the world's best tacos de sesos.

## DEAF

The inside of his ear had turned to cottage cheese. He tried elbowing his elbow in there, and grinding things out, because his doctor said that elbows were just the right size. He rooted around with a Q-Tip because his father said to do it. His father was blind, and Q-Tip instructions—on the box's reverse—have never been written in Braille. Soon, the telephone muttered when he answered, his mother's voice like the inside of a bag of cotton balls. He answered with the receiver curled to his other ear, but realized that, too, had filled with curds that smelled of what he would later learn was bacteria that grows in warm and moist places. That later was when he was sixteen and gloriously deaf, parked on the stretch of road straighter than the girl's brunette head, under the sky star-studded so that he hated the word "studded," and he was lonely.

# DEDICATION

For Sarah, my freak who found her freak

## DICEPHALIC PARAPAGUS

Dicaphalic parapagus is a form of conjoined twins that is commonly found in the United States of America. In one example, when first born came a stereo, wailing, squelching, blasting static. Then the doctor felt an arm, a head. The room filled with squeals of white noise. Nurses scampered, heels clacking the children off from the birthing room. Do you want to hold them? Their mother blubbered, knowing one day she'd shower them with love in the shape of water from the shower in her bathroom. And so they came: one body, two heads, the boy and the stereo. And the mother said my god what a gift what a miracle my god I will love you.

They learned to coordinate movement: the boy leaning toward an open window, the stereo squelching out and searching for a signal. There was the hint of man shoulders, squared, of a tape deck, a CD carousel. Sure, people stared and took photos. The television stations came in droves, demanding that they owed the world their story, because televisions cannot exist without stories.

Their tiny town, with the tiny market, with the tiny BP, on the tiny corner, across from their tiny school, accustomed itself to the boy and the stereo, how they played basketball, drove their car while other kids played their stations on their own stereos.

By senior year a change stormed through, the stereo pumping out rap, the boy screaming for punk rock,

Skynyrd, Golgotha, anything with guitars! The stereo bassed it up and the hip hop blasted out. The doctor said separation was impossible: separate hearts and lungs, distinct wiring, but a shared liver and intestines.

And the boys, despite their obvious musical differences, did not want to separate. Together and separate, they said, the stereo now blasting "I Tried" by Bone Thugs-N-Harmony, together and separate, the boy said, popping the collar of their Polo knit.

## DRUNK DRIVER

Every morning, in front of the bathroom mirror: the alphabet backwards. He watched flies zitting around in the filthy kitchen. He took the steps down the stoop on one foot. Every trip from couch-to-fridge-to-bathroom was done toe-to-heel, straight-lined.

He and his girlfriend were working to offset DUI inevitability. You'll see soon that this is not so much a story, but a rendition of everything that's expected.

Carrie and our man were always together, with the rest of their friends. Their training was why they ended up back at the apartment. They'd all leave the Pub, piled into the man's Jeep, and everyone would screech out, "To the Zephyr!" Some stupid punk band would be playing that Mike just had to see. The group would find themselves parked in the space at the apartment ten minutes later. Our hero had trained himself to autopilot home. Mike said, "There are artists and leaders of men, but Dave, Dave's gift: he can drink and drive."

Dave had gotten himself out of scrapes, once even high on crack. The cops pulled him over for a busted headlight he knew beforehand was gone, but Dave had chained himself to barstools for so long he hadn't had it fixed. Dave went into his zone. His heart rate dropped. He willed his pupils to un-dilate. The cop said, "What's the matter with your buddy?" That was Terrance. "Terrance is just scared of cops." The officer—he wore glasses, so

Dave knew he could out-lie him—said, "You seem fine to me, just get home and don't go out anymore tonight."

Now Dave wonders if Carrie's alive, what she's doing, who she's fucking, where she lives. Dave rides trains downtown, up to midtown, out to Harlem and Brooklyn. There's no use for a car in the city.

# EAGLE SCOUT

The following ranks denote the path a young man takes in a journey from boyhood to young adulthood, while as a Boy Scout in the Boy Scouts of America, an independent youth organization in the United States.

## The Rank of Boy Scout

Ten point five years. The belly rolls out like the shirt is watermelon-stuffed. The tennis shoes' lips (Reebok high tops) flop while walking. Hair is a massive helmet, and should the head meet—as it often will—the points of rocks, the mesh of curls act as cushion against damage. Girls are closed eyelids and open-mouthed laughter. Baseball—the one thing that makes the little bells toll—has only just begun to grow real. These uniformed kids and their salutes, their hiking boots, sting of the ridicule already suffered. One more way to slowly die will only speed the process.

## The Rank of Tenderfoot

The mud will cake along the shorts so that it resembles a butterfly's wings. The watch will slip from the wrist—time itself—lost along the rocks' sodden depths of a lagoon later to be poisoned. Oh, irony: a Boy Scout Camp under federal mandate for pollution control. The father will laugh and admonish, thinking, *my god*. The scoutmaster will smoke cigarettes and his sons—named Robert, Bob, Robert, and Bert—will pull at the skin of their necks making the red redder and the checked flannel will be a symbol of the scotch in the blood, the fear behind the eyes, the peanut butter and jelly sandwiches.

## The Rank of Second Class

The hand reaches the crotch. Not of the oak once scrabbled up while playing G.I. Joe and Star Wars, but *the* crotch. The hand has still skinned no other skin besides its own, outside of handshakes, hugs, chicken—that which peels back before indulging in the thigh. The television in the parents' bedroom skips from clear to static on sixteen, the Playboy Channel. This entices the hand crotchward. The hand learns things about gripping a pencil and scribbling irregularly the pages of a black and white speckled composition book.

## The Rank of First Class

The Mexicans (see *Mexicans*, pg. 81) have decided that not only are Boy Scouts idiots, but since they consist almost entirely of white boys, they are also stupid. The clothes—outside of uniform—in turn, have taken a decidedly Z Cavaricci turn. The collared shirt buttons button to the neck. The black suede Playboy loafers slip on. The hair, thickly moussed each morning post-shower, sweeps back, the mullet curling at the nape. Squiggling in a collection of merely three hundred strands down the forehead, equally moussed, the squiggles creepily stiff as a pencil, or as a subliminal arrow.

## The Rank of Star

An amazing thing has happened: The moths cocooned upon the oak branches have burst forth from their chrysalises and swirl the branches à la confetti. So, too, have the trousers ceased to be trousers and become pants. A crease along the thigh, down the ankle, becomes imperative. So is aftershave. Actual shaving happens only every fourth or fifth day, a routine never to be broken despite the scraggle of whiskers that weekly grow like billions of Jack's bean stalks, like billions of Jacks, which are ubiquitous, as omnipresent as football players. The mind has become a hive of breasts and breasts.

## The Rank of Life

The ranks are obsessive. Each higher rank lilts by, the future waving hello from the passenger window of a passing Dodge, or Chrysler. The Life Scout becomes a life scout at ten point five years. Later, it will be agreed that this was during the eleven point fifth year of life. The lashings have perfected, the two half-hitches, the sheepshank, the bowline (pronounced "Bow-lyn"). Pico Blanco—a mountain aptly topped white with quartz—remains ambitious. Ambition itself is a mountain. The mountain mountains up and the lungs suffer as much as the calves and balls and balls of feet. The rifles of the rifle range smoke and the smoke curls like a woman's hips, or her tongue, or the hump of a mountain.

## The Rank of Eagle

The girlfriend's Russian accent has tits with nipples that, when hard, are exactly like a baby's thumb between the fingers. This prompts the plants to strain and swell. Haircuts clip out the end of each bi-week. Under a weed haze the Little Sur River is a wisp of silver hair. The last rank is the door to a bar. The bar holds up a sign reading "We ID". The ID is the same as the collective soul of the river. The girlfriend's mouth claims the ID, the lips lipping around the D, closing up the I. This, ultimately, makes the girlfriend the enemy, and the bar a friend.

# ECTRODACTYLIC

An ectrodactylic is a human whose fingers and toes are fused and form claw-like appendages. In some instances ectrodactylics have performed in circus sideshows. In this particular example, the woman we're speaking of had a family. Each morning the teeth of her comb combed through the strands of her hair. Oatmeal was mostly what she and her family sucked up for breakfasts and, occasionally, on weekends there were pancakes. The children circled on their bottoms before Saturday cartoons. A husband, a man whose beard stubble could appear by five o'clock most days, hated the cliché five o'clock shadow and once fired himself from a job for squishing his knuckles through the coworker's face who mentioned it. This husband did this with his own fist. But this man went to therapy over the anger that his rapid hair growth aroused and he applied and interviewed and his new job put him into better checks at the end of every two weeks. And the woman held a productive job as a middle school teacher in the small county in California where this family dwelt. All of the other teachers and even the principal came for the cake they shelled out each year for said woman's birthday. This woman was an ectrodactylic and she dressed herself most naturally mornings with the sun spilling into her bedroom through the window. Before she quit smoking, often in her clawed hands one found a cigarette deftly handled, lit, and smoked from with ease. But now she merely pens her signature and other writing upon paper, and she maneuvers her modest compact front wheel drive about the family's modest town. This woman was not a circus performer and thus her life was quite normal. And that is what most humans on Earth are striving for.

## ENVIRONMENTALISTS

These humans have taken a political and ethical point of view and transformed it into a religion. Their chief deity is David Henry Thoreau, who, after undergoing a transformative experience (some have called it a "vision quest") upon a deserted lake shore, emerged changed even down to his name. Afterwards he went as Henry. Henry created a son who was not born, but evolved, and lived to spread the word of his evolution, Charles. Thus combined, the two holy texts of Environmentalism are *Walden* and *The Origin of Species*. Modern Environmentalists hold worship sometimes at the base of, and sometimes in the canopy of, rather large trees. Many Environmentalists take pilgrimages to their holy land of California, and can often be found in their holy city of San Francisco, although sizeable populations of environmentalists can be found in the states of Oregon and Washington, as well. Take, for instance, a particular Environmentalist found holding services at the base of a red maple just across the border in an I-5 rest area. He hugged this tree, pressing his cheek upon its bark until a bark interrupted his reverie, and the offending dog lifted a leg in salute of the man-tree the dog blissfully remained unaware of actually being two distinct and individual life forms. The Environmentalist has as one of his many commandments to not harm living creatures and thus the Environmentalist stared peacefully while the dog—a Scotch terrier—kicked up the grass to cover his deed. But walking back to his car—among the sins of this particular Environmentalist—the man could be heard issuing a stream of his lords' names used in vain: "David damned dog, motherfucking Darwin dammit pissed all over my fucking leg." And through this is revealed the many incongruities and contradictions that most organized religions are beset by.

## FANTASY NOVEL, THE

Here, the wizards are middle-aged instead of young or old, and they always stay middle-aged. They masturbate instead of having sex with their husbands and wives, and they're always dropping their kids off at wizard school, and saying every afternoon you will be staying with either your wizard father or your wizard mother, and no goddamit you cannot come over because it's wizard daddy's night, and that's his responsibility, goddamit. In the fantasy novel the knights' names are all "Night", so when someone lurks through darkened mines plagued by creatures fowler than the stench of this prose, everyone screams *Night, watch out!* And Night screams back, *I can't see anything!* And the princesses are whores, and the princes are frat boys, and their fraternity is called the Royal Fantasy Novel Nonesuch, and the magic is called god, and the lesser magic is also called god.

## FLEA AND SNAKE, THE

Only in rare instances will fleas seek nourishment for their recently-fertilized eggs from the blood of a snake. In one case, the roads that morning were a king snake's belly, oil and rainwater glazed. A flea drove along in his flea-sized Toyota. To say this flea drove we mean he slid. This is because king snakes are slimy—as are all snakes. To be technical, snakes become slimy only in metaphors, as when a television or film actor refers to another character as a "slimy snake." Snake's—literally—are only slimy when sneezed upon, or doused with olive oil. Attempting either of these is not recommended. Touch a king snake. It is not a pleasant experience. The arm hairs tingle and a shooting runs through the knee pits. Most prefer snakes in pictures, still or motion. Then again, a king snake eats other snakes, and thus is slightly more tolerable. There are not any king snakes in Georgia. These snakes one finds only in California, where the hills are gold and the grasses hide black and ivory striped bodies. This morning, the morning being spoken of, the flea was on its way to the snake's head—which is also known as a Federal Courthouse. At the snake's neck is where the blood is richest.

## FOOTBALL ANNOUNCERS (AMERICAN)

The American football announcer's favorite word is "football." Listen carefully while examining an American football contest. The quarterback cannot protect the ball in the pocket, nor the running back carry the ball upfield. Certainly, no wide receiver ever makes a spectacular catch of the ball. These, according to the American football announcer, the player can only properly do with a *foot*ball. Thus, the quarterback can really throw the football. The running back really knows how to tuck the football in so as not to fumble the football. That wide receiver sure can catch the football. In the history of the football game, no football pass has ever been completed out of bounds. Also, in order to win the football game, one or the other football team has to move the football downfield, and eventually put the football in the end zone. That's the only way one of these two football teams can win this football game. Football announcers are almost universally married to footballs. They kiss their football goodbye Sunday mornings on their way to the football stadium. In their football they listen to the football radio station, while stuck in the insufferable football traffic. If they could, they would make like a football player, and power their way through the line of footballs, blocking them from the goal of the football parking lot. Tailgating party here? Oh, footballs shuttle back and forth between football fans' fingers. Meantime, idling past, the football announcer calls each toss, each gently cupped football grab, he contemplates the fans' burgers and dogs, crossed legs from lowered trucks' tailgates. The football announcer parks his football, looks upon his football church, glaring in fall sunlight, and he chants: football, football, football, football, football. Try it. Come Superbowl Sunday. Football announcers cannot even spell baseball. Once, one learned to, and he was summarily dismissed from the football announcers' guild. It's said that this football announcer went on to discover the little known fourth law of thermodynamics: the football itself is equal to the football divided by the mouths uttering "football," multiplied by a variable representing the football fan. This variable represents the source of the universe's black holes.

# FOOTBALL ANNOUNCERS (EVERYWHERE ELSE)

Their favorite word is goooooooooaaaaaaaaalllllllllllll although singularly syllabic in most instances, this one syllable is impossible to utter with any brevity. Hence, although the announcer's favorite word, the far more commonly voiced "pass" trumps their favorite in presentation. One observes the football announcer's enthusiasm for their favorite noun to determine its primary position in their lexicon. The difficulty for football announcers arises in the simplicity of their syllables. Every noun, verb, adjective, pronoun, &c, is single-syllabic. Thus a football announcer's rendition of the contest's events resembles the sound of a human's fingers clacking away at a keyboard. Students mired in their respective areas of expertise at UCLA's Dick Butkus's College of Sports Announcers hear these football announcers in neighboring labs and assume them to be prolific writers. They are, in fact, excellent communicators in Morse Code. Thus a few seconds of the football announcer's genius: dash dash dot, dash dash dash, dash dot, dash dash dot dot, dot dash, dot dash dot dot dot, dot, dot dot dot    dot dash dash dot, dot dash, dot dot dot, dot dot dot    dash dash dash dash    dash dot, dash dash dash, dash dot, dash dash dot dot, dot dash, dot dash dot dot dot, dot, dot dot dot dash dash dot, dash dash dash dash dash dash dash dash dash dash dash dash dash dash dash dash dash, dot dash dot dash dot dash dot dash dot dash dot dash dot dash dot dash, dot dash dot dot dot dash dot dot dot dash dot dot dot dash dot dot dot dash dot dot dot dash dot dot dot dash dot dot!!!!!!!! Transliterated this comes out: "Gonzales passes to Gonzales, gooooooooaaaaaaaa allllllllllllll!!!!! And when put into context, the football announcer has determined he will have bacon with his scrambled eggs instead of the turkey sausage, because it's gameday, and he might as well treat himself.

## FREAKS

The compilers of this volume have undertaken a bold task in defining the various types and accompanying characteristics of Freaks. In doing so a definition of Freaks must be determined in order to establish the veracity of such a presumptuous thesis, all in direct compliance with the appeasement of critics of the present volume. Freaks consist of various types and subcategories: namely Freaks of the Freak Movement of the late 1960s and into the early 1970s, the subsequent monikering of analog telephone tamperers and early digital computer hackers under the alternate portmantueau-ish spelling Phreakers (the portmanteau it should be briefly noted has characteristics similar to Voltron and various Autobot and Decepticon combined Transformers, in that the portmanteau consists of combined words. But we digress), and later Freaks are associated with the 1970s proliferation of the pornographic industry due to Rick James's gold record-selling hit "Superfreak." Subsequently, the use of Freak has been attributed to humans with unusual lifestyle, stylistic, and body-altering choices. Hence, "Freak" has been attributed to those of the Pierced and Tattooed, to those of dyed and dreadlocked hair (note the overlapping), and of those bearing platformed shoes. In recent years Freak has been used in jocular circles to refer to one's friends and loved-ones, as in, *You're such a freak*. As such, Freak can be defined as nearly any and all humans as they exist on Earth.

## FRONT MATTER

This Book was written for one purpose and one purpose only: So that readers will become aware of, and respect the existence of, Freaks in the reader's everyday existence. The compilers and editors have no illusions about this book being used as a reference tool. They expect you to use this book, make love on top of it when it's been left on your bed and forgotten in the passionate sweep of general missives to the floor at such times, and they expect you will often spill your beer upon it. After you have learned about Freaks, you can throw this book away. Along the way, the compilers and editors hope you will have acquired a copy of the *Freak-In-Training Reference Manual* to use throughout your career.

This book is not intended as a reference tool, because you cannot use it in everyday life, nor in the continual examination of the nearly constant influx of Freaks one will encounter.

In the course of choosing specific types to be classified as "freaks" specific criteria must be considered. Therefore in keeping with current scientific and philosophic trends toward human classification, the criteria are as follows: 1) Is the subject alive, living, breathing, cells dividing and dying? 2) Does the subject make use of—directly or indirectly—a form of complex linguistics? 3) The subject must have at least one of the requisite following characteristics for life forms in the known universe: response to external stimuli, the capability for reproduction, general homeostasis, and the ability to grow and respond to changes in external environments, i.e., to adapt.

Because this book was designed with such care and attention to detail, the options for its use are necessarily limited. Upon its inception, the following uses were taken into consideration:

• You should study every subject in this book. To diffuse the knowledge of FREAKS, is the professed design of the following work. What methods, it may be asked, have the compilers employed to accomplish this design? Not to mention original articles, they have had recourse to the best books upon almost every subject, extracted the useful parts, and rejected whatever appeared trifling or less interesting. Instead of dismembering the FREAKS of Earth, by attempting to treat them intelligibly under a multitude of technical terms, they have digested the principles of every FREAK in the form of systems or distinct treaties, and explained the terms as they occur in the order of the alphabet, with references to the classifications to which they belong.

• As this plan differs from that of all the Dictionaries of Arts and Sciences hitherto published, the compilers think it necessary to mention what they imagine gives it superiority over the common method. A few words will answer this purpose. Whoever has had occasion to consult

Terwilliger, Owens, &c. or even the voluminous French *Encyclopedie*, will have discovered the folly of attempting to communicate FREAKS under the various technical terms arranged in an alphabetic order. Such an attempt is repugnant to the very idea of Science, which is a connected series of conclusions deduced from self-evident or previously discovered principles. It is well if the reader be capable of comprehending the principles and relations of the different parts of FREAKS, when laid before her in one uninterrupted chain. But where is she who can learn the principles of any FREAK from a dictionary compiled upon the plan hitherto adopted? We will, however, venture to affirm, that any reader of ordinary parts, may, if he chooses, learn the principles of the Action Film, of Americans, of those with Big Legs, of Celebrities, &c. &c. from THE BOOK OF FREAKS.

• You need to decide on a study schedule. The compilers separated the subjects and chose the quantity of FREAKS in this book so that you can easily review a chapter in an hour or so—even if you are taking other courses with other work. There are ninety-one chapters in the following work. So, you need at least fifteen study days. The compilers recommend a plan to take every fourth or fifth study day off. Use the days off to rest, review, and study FREAKS in their natural habitats. If you are pressed for time, you don't have to take the days off. That remains your choice.

The editors, though fully sensible of the propriety of adopting the present plan, were not aware of the length of time necessary for the execution, but engaged to begin the publication too early. However, by the remonstrances of the compilers, the publication was delayed for twelve months. Still time was wanted. But the subscribers pushed the editors, and they at last persuaded the compilers to consent to the publication. If time had been allowed, the compilers designed to have completed the sciences before proceeding to the technical terms; and by that means to have guarded against omission, and made all the references from the terms to FREAKS more particular. The consequence was unavoidable.

We must further acknowledge, that, in some instances, we deviated from the general plan; but, we hope, not without reason. For example, under the headings Courtship and Human, it would have been endless, and perhaps a useless task, to have given the generic distinctions of every wink or date, and of all human aspects. These are to be found under the names of the specifics themselves.

With regard to errors in general, whether falling under the denomination of mental, typographical, or accidental, we are conscious of being able to point out a greater number than any critic. Men who are acquainted with the innumerable difficulties attending the execution of a work of such an extensive nature will make proper allowances. To these we appeal, and shall rest satisfied with the judgment they pronounce.

## FUCKERS

Contrary to one of the Oxford English Dictionary's definitions of the singular version of this noun, fuckers are very rarely engaged in the act of fucking.

## GIGANTOMASTIA

Humans who suffer from this condition experience rapid and unusual growth of the breasts. That is not what actually concerns the compilers of this volume. What does interest us is the fact that Soleil Moon Frye, the child star famous for her role as Punky Brewster, is among the few sufferers of this connective tissue disease. To be honest, even that fact is not what really concerns us, not so much as the fact of the existence of Punky Brewster. Punky Brewster was a character who epitomized the burgeoning emotional and psychological strength of females in popular media portrayals in the 1980s. We are also surprised that television executives did not see the verisimilitude of such writing and performances until the 1980s. All this said, the title of this entry should not go unnoticed. If you have not viewed images of Punky Brewster prior to breast reduction, then you again will be impressed at the strength of character required to carry such a burden. Gigantomastia can cause considerable pain and discomfort. Finally, though, what truly designates Punky Brewster a Freak, is the actress who breathed her to life: Soleil Moon Frye. She remains happily married and a mother to two children who suffer from celebrity name syndrome. Regardless, instinctively, Soleil Moon Frye is by all accounts a good mother.

## GIFTS

Gifts are commonly given on special occasions, such as birthdays and anniversaries, and are a common trope found in quest narratives. For example, in this narrative the cliffs cliffed out of the ocean and mountained up. In the gullies giant redwoods tossed shade over the king fern and sorrel. At the gate, the people in this narrative met an old man with hair like whipped cream around his ears and skin like a raisin's, though he looked less than appetizing. His glasses were as white as the fog.

The old man said to the first traveler: "This is the Map of Ventana. Use it to find your way." The traveler took the old, unfolded map and gazed across its fading lines.

The old man gave to the second traveler a glass with moisture condensed upon it. The old man said, "The water is deliciously cold—straight from the Little Sur River. See how refreshing it is." The traveler, indeed, felt as fresh as when she had awakened that morning.

To the third traveler the old man said, "In the wilderness there are no bathrooms. Be sure you have your own paper." And he passed over the roll of Charmin, saying, "Please don't squeeze the Charmin."

It was then the travelers recognized Mr. Whipple. "You're great, Mr. Whipple!" the travelers exclaimed, in thanks for the gifts.

And Mr. Whipple sent the travelers, thus armed, into the wilds of Ventana.

## GIRLS

Girls are young female humans with smelly feet. Not all humans suffer from smelly feet, but this is a singular fact about girls. Over time, girls learn to overcome this chromosomal disorder after having discovered the fact of their odoriferous podia. Some girls achieve womanhood and thus by this stage have thrown the cover back over their stinky feet and therefore have disguised themselves to men and/or other women in order to make themselves more selectable in the courtship process. Girls are also known for being doo-doo heads and booger faces. No, but seriously. Girls suffer from this sort of boyishness from most boys. Girls, in real life, are humans who live on a primarily patriarchal planet. Girls who became women strove for suffrage in the United States of America, achieving it only with that nation's 19$^{th}$ Amendment to their Constitution in 1920. Imagine that! A line of women before the White House, bundled against the windless day, the snow clinging to the leather soles of their leather shoes, their faces worn and tanned by summer and winter sun. And one woman, at attention, her dead son's WWI soldier's helmet tilting on her curled head, no smile. Her name is probably Beatrice. Beatrice was a mother, and a wife, and a human who lived and ate, and reproduced, and died on planet Earth. The state of Mississippi ratified the 19$^{th}$ Amendment on March 22$^{nd}$ 1984.

## GRAPHIC NOVEL, THE

Here, every graphic panel looks like this:

Look closely and you'll find a snow-covered field. Very little happens, though critics universally praise its poetics.

## GUITARIST, THE

is a college-aged male who has learned to play this musical instrument as a courtship rite. Typically, the guitarist hears the whisp of a riff, a classically-rendered trickle. This, the budding guitarist decides, will surely get him laid. He then turns to the Blues, knowing full well that melancholy inspires pity, that pity engenders compassion, that within the word compassion lies passion. Unfortunately, the guitarist will attempt his own ditties, the titles of which are all single nouns: "Air" is a song about dolphins; "Cement," a sonneta of lost butterflies. The guitarist makes a narrative turn. Native American lore proves helpful, whilst staring at the granite upon the cliffs that cliff out from the north of the college campus. This princess that flung herself to her death at her lover's feet, that tale—which the guitarist has titled "Alpine"—will get him a pair of pink panties to fold. Eventually, the guitar grows dust and spider webs. The strings rust and snap each rarely strummed occasion. The guitarist becomes a retail outlet manager. His wife and children love him dearly.

## HANGNAIL, A

When you find this loose piece of skin on your fingertips, rip it back, the skin trickle rippling the forearm. A blood globe reflects irises, blue, and with the surrounding eye whites, think of July 4$^{th}$: the fog-dappled Marina beach sand that wound its way up the shorts and ground the thigh skin to tenderized red. That fucking surfer asshole with teeth for a head said, "You walk like you've got a stick up your ass." Knives slipped into pants and stones hefted at Ford pickups zipping past the walked route homeward from the school bus stop. That sleeveless jean jacket cocksucker's hair dripping mullet grease popped a zit when the blade flicked his wrist and the slice welled red. The stickiness congealing like a hangnail. The wife says, lotion-up, Vaseline that shit. Think of Steinbeck's Lenny, Lenny breaking Curly's hand in his own crumpling fist. Lenny was a big ill-witted boy who liked to pet soft things and usually killed them. That's what kind of retard to be. That's a retard.

## HAVES, THE

Haves can be found in most nations across planet Earth. There are some exceptions, primarily among the populations of sub-Saharan Africa. Despite their geographic variety, Haves share certain particular characteristics. The Haves voted for the other guy, they'll have you know. They always do. In nations where voting is more drama than nonfiction (note: this occurs in *all* nations) Haves are known to side with the other guy ideologically, but put their money and their mouths into factories that manufacture digital polling machines. Haves are found saddling the rear seats of vehicles from the following manufacturers: Cadillac and Mercedes. No self-respecting Have will be driven in anything Japanese—not even Japanese Haves. Haves have favorite cities, such as New York, and favorite verbs, like "to have." Haves will say, Have you been to New York City? They don't have restaurants in your city like they have in New York City. Have you seen the new Cadillac? I have. Haves never confuse the verb "to have" with the verb "to halve". You'll never find them saying, Let's halve this hot dog, or, We should halve this Mercedes. The verb "to cut", however, in certain contexts, is among the Have's favorites. Especially when it comes to one or the other of guys for whom they may or may not choose to vote. It all depends on who plans to cut taxes, or to cut welfare to the Have Nots, or to cut commercial time down during the Super Bowl. In this way, Haves are a perpetual contradiction, a living paradox, and so Haves have been and remain enigmatic studies for Science.

## HAVE NOTS, THE

Have Nots are not usually seen, but smelled. Follow a path of reeking patchouli and one finds—huddled on a streetside curb, smoking a grape-flavored bidi cigarette, right hand open and pleading for change or "buds," left hand strumming back a wayward dreadlock—the Have Not. Have Nots can also be recognized by their particular call which sounds eerily and exactly the same as *Hey bro, can I get a ride?* Not all Have Nots are true Have Nots, but are actually Haves in disguise. Sometimes Haves wish that they were actually Have Nots. For example, some Haves find their way to college campuses where they pick up the guitar (see *Guitarist, The*, pg. 64) and subsequently attempt to foil esteemless females with their wooing cadences about water, or waterfalls, or rivers, or lakes, and the dreamy shores thereupon. These impostors are not actually Have Nots, but Haves that have been seduced by the romantic legend surrounding Have Nots. While these Haves say to you, *sorry, brother, I haven't any change*, they are, at the same time, found cellphoning their Have parents while said Have parents meander a Mercedes or Cadillac around a metropolis peopled primarily by those in between the Haves and Have Nots (see *Human, A*, pg. 70). True Have Nots are in fact quite a rarity in North America and Europe, but can be found in vast numbers on all the other of Earth's continents. The true Have Nots of a subcontinent such as India can also be found puffing a bidi, but as opposed to dreadlocks, what little hair they may have is turbaned under a turban. The Have Nots of Sub-Saharan Africa are in pursuit of potable water, as opposed to the North American variety of the faux Have Not, who is in constant search for the next jam band. All artificial Have Nots are fans of jam bands.

## HIGH LIFE

The man with the High Life was born in August, the second cruelest month. Soon after, photos of him swaddled in dazzling white imitation sheepskin speckled the halls. His childhood was idyllic: artichoke fields and strawberry wars, an endless oak forest. His father spanked him only once: he shat upon the hall carpet. Prior to this movement he wondered—yes, he *remembers* this—why must this necessary thing occur in the tiny plastic basin in the bathroom? He gnawed through pouches of Big League Chew. The Mexicans giggled at his stunted *español*, his squiggled hair, à la Squiggy. The high school football team's mascot was the Condors, colors silver and black. Every Mexican gangbanger on the team imagined himself an Oakland Raider. The man with High Life coated his British Knights with cheap white leather repair. Freshman year of college Kurt Cobain's brains met the bird shot in his twelve gauge. The fraternity told this man to quit sucking down bong loads. His Greek PhD. pal said that Nietzsche's free spirits might free—or master—him. This Panamanian chick sent the man with High Life masturbating for years. He drank only Bushmills—later Jameson. Fuck snowboarding. His tattoos are tattoos of his own skin. Camel Wides gave way to Lights, to air, and a girlfriend. That stint with Atlanta's cocaine made the man with High Life's stories turn gray. He found a diamond, and in the grocery store's breadcrumbs aisle, his bent knee suggested, *marriage?* Since, his cat is nearly dead from cancer, his mailbox piles with rejections and RSVPs, tonight there's chili to microwave. He is drinking High Life.

## HUMAN, A

Humans are born normal—like most mammal infants, head first. This human grew to a normal eighteen years: knit collared shirt, chinos, deck shoes toggled to his toes. Inside, past the ruddy hair strands, and briny scalp, under the thinning layers of epidermis and fat, under the skull sewn and fused in its casements, under the pitted and wrinkled gray matter, the pituitary gland's tumor, the pituitary gland itself, the epiphyseal plate sealed, squeezed out growth hormone molecule after growth hormone. His headaches were trains in the tiniest under-road New York Subways, his shoes, stretched beyond decks capable of holding them. He grew like hands stretching out toward some god. He grew and no one wanted to see him, a Goliath to everyone's David. He endured and today he drives a truck.

# INDEX

S



---

T



---

U



---

V



---

W



---

Y



---

Z

## JAPANESE, THE

What the Japanese love more than anything: squid ice cream. It started after the Great Kantō Earthquake of 1923 leveled Tokyo, collapsing the loading bay doors to Emiko's ice cream, just across Shin-Ohashi Dori from Nihonbashi fish market. Fresh market squid poured out, flowing through the Tokyo streets in a river of squid and vanilla, churning up the ramen and curried beef vendors, along with the then-few automobiles. Due to the ensuing earthquake-driven famine, Emperor Taishō declared Tokyo a disaster zone, and forced rationing when into effect. The residents scoured the street, licking, slurping every last ounce of squid and ice cream, leaving the then-few chrome bumpers shining, and later streetlights were erected, electricity flowed again through the overhead wires, the Emperor declared war against the Chinese. Everyone grew prosperous and bought gallons of squid ice cream. Emiko and his ice cream shop resurrected and now there's a photo of him on the wall, an old man, standing next to Elvis Presley, the second most beloved thing in Japan.

## JERKS

This is the pseudo-scientific classification for members of law enforcement in the city of Denver, Colorado. The correct appellation for these individuals is Pigs, however, the volume's compilers have exhausted the entries under "P", and have therefore striven to endure in other areas of the English alphabet. Thus, Jerks are known for their totalitarian demeanor and their flat-top haircuts. Most jerks can be seen sporting Kevlar in the middle of malls, downtown streets, and in the lobbies of many of Denver's upscale hotels. Should you find yourself sauntering down a Denverian quay and you are accosted by a Jerk, it is likely because you are an African, African American, Mexican, Mexican American—basically anything other than Caucasian American—or, you might appear to be white, but god forbid your lips lisp anything other than the most Midwestern of accents. In such instances, Jerks are likely to ask you, *where are you going, where have you been*, despite their lack of knowledge concerning the short fictions of Joyce Carol Oates, American fiction writer born June 16th 1938. In fact, you would be in trouble, too, if you looked like Joyce Carol Oates, since she carries a distinctively intellectual demeanor, and Jerks are well-known for their dislike of smarty-smarties. Jerks prefer people like them, whom they'll have you know, are *Americans* (pg. 7). As we have already demonstrated, this is among the unfortunate side effects of Americans.

## LEGLESS MAN

Today you crossed your legs while eating your sandwich, while the legless man—clearly a veteran: tattooed, grizzled gray beard—chewed along jabbering at you. Your irises had wandered over where his legs had been, outside the downtown train station for nearly a year now, his stumps swaddled, pant legs tucked up like enormous skeins of yarn. He always gripped the Styrofoam cup and said nothing, his fingers fluttering a hello, palm raised, a salute to every commuter heeling their clackety ways to and from some paycheck dungeon. Today you bought him ham and salami on wheat, mayo, lettuce, onion, and bell pepper. Salt and vinegar. You now regret that you were also kind enough to chew next to him, your right knee atop your left, adjacent the air swimming with molecules where the cells of this man's legs once took up space. Your own sandwich—turkey—sweats in your fingers, while the man's babble over choppers and an airlift leave you thinking of him. Not this man, the veteran. But you know who we're talking about, your man at home, the man just returned, only just now slipping sweatpants past his hips in your apartment, and the photos of himself, those he sent, where he clutches a machine gun, posing in his urban camo with children's brown smiles, and their little hands that grip the candy he'd gifted. You reach for your pant leg and brush away a few crumbs that fell there, clinging to the fabric.

## LITERARY NOVEL, THE

This novel is usually titled as such: *The Physicist's Wife's Water for Pachyderms Collectors' Son's Amazing Adventures with Clay*. The main character in the literary novel is always a mafia hit man with a soft side for My Little Pony, because his little sister used to play with My Little Pony, but she was gunned down by the neighborhood white boys—with rubber bands—and by neighborhood it is assumed that what is actually meant is suburb. The main character's name is Adam, and he also used to be a straight-edge punk. Now he's thinking about joining the priesthood, but what will happen when his past catches up with him? Will his suburb come back to haunt him with terrifying flying mini vans? Will his collars refuse to pop upon command? Someone offers him a drink? Only love can tell in this Penguin-Harper-Little-Brown-Algonquin-Houghton-Mifflin-FSG blockbuster with the straight to DVD film version glued to the inside cover and also soon to found at Blockbuster. All of the music is by Coldplay, except for the music that is by Wilco.

## LOST, THE

There are two ways: on the left, a Shell gas station sprouting black men in rags with greasy fingers, tire-mending men with waxed plugs thrust in their trouser pockets; on the right, a dilapidated thrift store, its televisions complete with digital readouts of the channels. The Lost claim that there is one choice, that our argument is a logical fallacy. We say fallacies are fallacies, that only those who care about such things are the Lost. They make television programs for the Lost. The trick is, is that it is the Lost who are lost, not the characters portrayed on such television programs. If the Lost will look this up they'll find that these are truisms: the Shell gas station and the thrift store. Once the Lost make a decision they invariably opt for the thrift store, where they find a paperback edition of Forster's *Passage to India*. This volume will be on sale for one penny.

## MALDIVIANS

Maldivians are inhabitants of Maldives, and coexist with an influx of dragonflies and babies, both of which originate only in the Maldives, and migrate thousands of miles only to return a few months later for a short stay before moving off again forever. This is "what we call life." Compounding this breed-and-flee tendency, the Maldivians do not cultivate hops and thus have no beer. Poor Maldives! In an effort to counteract this deficiency Maldivians have attempted a beer brewed from babies and dragonflies. Unfortunately, this resulted in a plethora of monocled and top-hatted Monopoly men. Maldivians cannot stand Monopoly and rightly attempted an export of the overstock to Burma where it is claimed that the Monopoly men behaved largely like that actor from *Easy Rider*. The Maldives have no mountains and thus the word for mountain in Maldivian is green. There is an abundance of green in the Maldives, and Maldivians climb these mountains, plumbing them for views of the blue lagoons, and from these heights they dream of storm surges and of fishless fishing boats.

## MAN ON A TRAIN

This kind of man leans into one's book-pointed face and screeches about shutting the fuck up. In most cases, the eyes of the accused become surprise. Said book's title spells out the letter "S," also "Is," as well as "for Suspense." The accused jumps out of the seat. But this man—the Polo aftershave and Phillies reek reeking off his Polo shirt—swings and the braking car rocks everyone back, eyebrows clear of knuckles. The book-reader's forehead destroys the man on the train's nose. His nose becomes a rose that rolls upon the train's flooring leaving smears of rose all over the cheap plastic-ness. Fingers find their way into roses. Unfortunately for the man on the train, our book-reader's Chuck Taylors also kick at said roses. Then the doors wheeze open, and the man on a train is never seen again.

## MEXICANS

A Mexican is an inhabitant of Mexico, a country axiomatically hexed by *brujas* since the dawn of clichés. The Mexican's favorite Mexican word is Mexico. Variations on this word abound in the Mexican lexicon. Mexicans are fond of saying, for example, *Mexico is one really great place, especially for Mexico*, or, *Let us go then, you and I, to Mexico*. Despite this last homeward bound-sounding phrase, Mexicans are almost completely confined to Mexico. For example, there are next to zero Mexicans in Russia. Next to that: a series of Asian and Eastern European countries that equally house zero Mexicans. Poor inhabitants of the Eurasian Steppe! They have never suckled tacos brimming with *mixiote*! Mexicans comprise the world's largest owners and players of tubas. In the Mexican household one finds a profusion of tubas unmatched anywhere else on Earth. For a bed, the Mexican dreams away inside the large flared bell of a tuba. Mexicans have sixteen hands and six feet. The rapid movement makes photographing Mexicans particularly difficult, and few have been documented. What is known is that Mexicans suffer from the following bodily debilitations, expressed in their native tongue by the following respective pining declarations: they are constantly having their hearts broken, (*¡Ay, me rompas el Corazón!*); their bodies left cold (*¡dejas mi cuerpo tan frio!*); and are left to live without their loves (*¡dejame vivir sin tu amor!*). Despite this, Mexicans are extremely happy, as evidenced by the profusion of bright color in their style of dress. Mexicans' favorite color is tequila,

their favorite movie is *Mad Max Beyond Thunderdome*,
their favorite thing to do is sing in welcome to visitors,
chanting *bienvenidos, encantada, bienvenidos*.

## MOTHERS

Scream, "Clean up!" upstairs—still.

## MOUNTAIN LION

The mountain lion can be found on city streets in the dark early morning of weekend days. The cabs will have nearly ferried him home when a club sandwich calls out. That is, the drunken pit of the mountain lion's gut talks the language of club sandwiches.

Afterwards, on his walk from the diner, Jay Top steps a block, unwittingly, with the mountain lion, his arm cathetered for diabetes, or some other story. Jay Top says to the mountain lion, "I know you, don't I?"

Canines get bared, which are exactly like Jay Top's, except that the mountain lion's are in his mouth.

When Jay Top's palm finds the mountain lion's chest, stopping him, he says, "Now let's have your money."

Next comes a smile. "You don't really want that," says the mountain lion.

Down Peachtree the headlights are always twin mammal eyes floating in the nebulous skyscraper glow. Jay Top's knife glints across the asphalt, then the white concreted sidewalk.

A growl like the club sandwich hadn't been enough growls out. The mountain lion is about the size of an adult mountain lion. He hisses and spits as he rips off his t-shirt.

## MYSTERY STORY, THE

In the mystery story, we know that some dude is always the killer. The woman's body is found in the living room. The clues that led the hero to these discoveries are the following: a Bowie knife; the blood smearing the blade; a single hair, curling like a worm, deposited on the woman's backside; the tablespoon of semen. The real mystery was our detective going home where his wife's arms flapped like immensely thick twin flags while she stirred the ground beef in the frying pan. His daughter in her bedroom, kicking up her heels while telephoning her girlfriend, a freckled girl named Anna. The inevitable sound of the daughter's water pick for the bits of nightly meat she squirted from her braces. The uneasy sense that what these people needed was a murder mystery, that nothing about their lives is safe, that at any moment, the pine in their front yard might wrench from the earth, igniting in the subsequent electrical fire, that the pine falls to crush them, that their flesh will burn away.

## NE'ER DO WELL

The ne'er do well can be found trouncing the boulevards of cities near architecturally unsound buildings that are not quite but almost influenced by the Spanish, and that house primarily the Blind (see *Blind* pg. 14). Ne'er do wells sport trousers hiked to chin height, a style that ne'er do wells say to one another, is "bully." Should you upset the ne'er do well in the midst of his phonograph's rendition of Odeon's *Nutcracker* with your rambunctious whipper-snapper's rap, the ne'er do well shakes a balled fist your way, exclaiming "Why I oughtta!" To this the reply—to the ne'er do well in his natural habitat—is "Yeah, you and what army?" This has been classified as the ne'er do well's *call and response*. This will be what the ne'er do well will call a fine song and dance. Supposing, though, that you're wrong about your judgments, the ne'er do well will inquire what the repercussions might be should the ne'er do well call you a lunkhead. You will suppose that one of these days it's gonna be a smack to the moon. The lunkheaded ne'er do well will tell you that this is horseradish, and you will say, no, no, ne'er do well, even on the moon ne'er do wells cannot breathe any kind of atmosphere. Even on the moon, ne'er do well, all anyone sees is a dim vision of the Earth. The ne'er do well will ask you what you got to say about it. The correct response at this moment is to have your fists orbit each other while you mutter, "I'll say plenty."

## NEW YORK CITIANS

This moniker is meant to denote the inhabitants of North American's most populous metropolis from the citizens of the second most peopled state of those be-tagged "United of America." For example, the oft-cited "New Yorker" means nothing when attempting to differentiate between a human from Brooklyn and one from New Greece. And so, an effort to describe those members of the above entry is hereby attempted: All New York Citians, when one visits their environment, sound like this:

No dime nada de la coc—ya miter fuc—shup—man fuck Hitler—yo dude I don't think—hey what's yo—beeeeee eeeeeeeeeeeeeeeeeeeeeeeeeeeeeeeeeeeeeeeeeeeeeep—I wanna wha—I wanna wha—I wanna shoe—I'll take your goddamn—you can't park—no—no—no—we don't have that—we're out of tha—we don't have

. . . This is insufferable and tiring. It's an amazing feat of logistics that anything ever gets done in New York City, since all the humans must be terribly underslept.

## NOTE ON THE COMPILERS

The compilers of THE BOOK OF FREAKS live in Atlanta, Georgia. The compilers were born on the west coast of North America, in California, near San Francisco, and thus retain some of the characteristics of the San Franciscan. As a matter of ethos, the compilers are currently professors of composition, literature, and creative writing. They are the authors of a previous volume, PROSE. POEMS. A NOVEL., published in 2009 by Orange Alert Press. Their prose and poetry has appeared in literary magazines such as *The Chattahoochee Review*, *The Literary Review*, and *Copper Nickel*, among others. It should be noted that beginning in the fourth grade, and carrying on into high school, the compilers suffered from a debilitating disease called Cholesteatoma, a tumor that eats away at the ossicles of the middle ear, and that can eventually eat away the layer of skull separating the ear from the brain, thus exposing the brain to potential infection. The compilers are consequently sufficiently deaf, which has been a nuisance to their wife. Said wife of the compilers works as a lawyer, an occupation for which clarity has always been an issue. However, the wife remains loving, for which the compilers are eternally grateful. Information about the compilers can be found at jamieiredell.blogspot.com.

## O: THE WORLD: OF O

O is an international imperial force that since 1986 has spread so that today the sun never sets upon it. The driving propaganda of this terrorist entity has been through popular media such as a televised religious rite, a book club, and a magazine, *O*. It is noted that the breakfast cereal Cheerios is also a cleverly disguised message propagated by O. O, for the life of the compilers of this volume, we strive to forget the letter O. However, O has carved a future ripe with Os. At the University of O young women fresh from family rooms piped full of the sonorous voice of O major in seismographicotology: the analysis of visual representations of O impact on plate tectonics. These women will go on to write theses on the restorative qualities of O to victims of Rwandan genocide or children abandoned to the state. Later, they'll take on an editorship at *O*—possibly O director—and tally the number of times O appears on the cover of *O*: 13,872,653. By now we have abandoned everything but O. One cannot ignore the fact the even the planet, when spied from the surface of our distant moon, is an immense and blue hole-less O. We bow low to O and sing *O, O, O*. Men, like your humble compilers, will be O so sensitive—never avoiding the opportunity for a comment on how good every wife looks in her jeans, never slipping an accidental Lean Cuisine into the grocery cart full of frozen pozole, always renewing her subscriptions, the DVR always programmed to record every afternoon, some specified Standard Time.

## OLD BACK, THIS

Once hefted cinderblocks.

## PEOPLE NAMED SPENCER AND THEIR WIVES

The Spencers almost always wear fishing caps and, appended to those fishing caps, buttons proclaiming the Spencer's political views, which are as complex as "I dislike the idea of collectivism," or "perhaps a gun could solve the immediate issue between us." The caps and the buttons and the views upon said buttons are not nearly as offensive as these Spencers' wives. Such wives are continually out of breath, exasperated by the fact that most other humans do not agree with and so upset these wives' delicate sensibilities. Example: a Spencer's wife believes that one must always slice an orange, that stripping away the rind for later zesting is useless and a time-suck and energy waster. She believes one might simply reduce the juice of the store-bought orange variety, thus gaining the intensely focused and desired orange flavor. Even discussing the possibilities of a rindless orange, the wedges peeled away and eaten whole, will make a Spencer's wife squirm in her airline seat, should she be a passenger directly in front of others holding such a discussion pertaining to peeled oranges. Spencers' wives have an irresistible urge to relate to everyone the wrongs of their point of view. This inevitably results in the majority of humans telling a Spencer's wife that she can go fuck herself, thus causing the ubiquitous hypertension among the wives of people named Spencer. The Spencers, during all of this, remain gloriously ignorant of their wives' peculiar temperament and condition, and are equally uninformed about everything else on Earth. Example: Spencers have a ludicrous sense of history. For Spencers, the universe formed in the wake of General Sherman's march northward to Alaska, burning a hell on his way to the North Pole, capturing that stronghold for President Ulysses S. Grant. Due to this and other notions, when one meets another named Spencer, one sees that these humans perpetually stand mouth agape, expectant, asking for yet another Coca Cola, because one more Coca Cola is all you have to bring them and then your day is finished. Spencers have been the cause of approximately sixty-two percent of all known human wars.

## PEOPLE WHO WALK ON THEIR HANDS, THE

These humans all have at least one callus. Not all of their calluses live on their hands. Some have sprouted upon their elbows, or suburbed the tips of their thumbs. Some say these calluses rubbed to life inside their heads—the heads of the people who walk on their hands. These people—those who walk on their hands—tell us the history of us, for we were all once also people who walked on our hands. If you were to peer closely at the aforementioned calluses—to do this, you'd need a microscope—you would find other, tiny people who also walk on their hands, who themselves have tiny calluses. You could say that all these hand-walking people are analogous to you and me. Either way, we are all of us very tired.

## PET SITTING

GETTING TO THE APT.:

If you're coming from Riverside, you'll want to turn onto Magnolia. So, if you're coming from north to south on Riverside, that means you'll want to turn right onto Magnolia; if you're coming from south to north, take a left. If you're coming in on I-75, you'll want to get off at the Downtown exit. If you get to the Cemetery Road exit, you've gone too far. That's all if you're coming from south to north on 75. If you're coming from north to south on 75, still take the Downtown exit, but don't go so far that you reach the junction with 16, because then you've gone too far. Once you take the exit (the Downtown exit), you'll want to take a right or a left, depending on which direction you exited the freeway from. If you came in from south to north, then you want to take a left when you get to the light. If you came from north to south, take a right.

Once you get to Magnolia, my building will be on your left, at the end of the block. It's a seven-storey brick building. But, if you come at night you probably won't be able to make out the bricks, or how tall the building is (there are lots of trees!), so look for the drug store on the right at about the middle of the street. It's a CVS, and next door is a Blockbuster. The Blockbuster and CVS are only about fifty yards from my building, which will be on the left. You can park on the street from 10 AM to 4 PM for two hours before you get a ticket. But if you come during rush hour (between 6 AM and 9 AM and from 4 PM to 6 PM) you won't be able to park at all, and your car will be towed. But if you come really early (before 6 AM) or late (after 6 PM) you won't have to worry about parking at all. But, Sinamyn doesn't like to have visitors that early or late, so I recommend not coming during those times. Also, as for the parking, Magnolia's not exactly a "safe" street during those hours, so if you park, be sure not to leave any valuables in plain sight, and I'd just leave the doors unlocked, so that the homeless don't break any windows before they riffle through your things. Once, I parked on the street and returned and found syringes on the floorboards and I'd only been parked down there for like twenty minutes!

Once you get to the front of the building (the address is 419, FYI; I know you've been here before, but, just to be safe!), look to the left, on the brick wall (here you'll actually be able to see the bricks—even at night, because of the street lamps. They're really old, aren't they?), which will be west of the main door. There's a telephone dialing pad sort of thing there. Dial *0265, which will unlock the front door. Then you can get inside. Inside, there will be a hallway to the left, but don't go down that. To your right is the staircase. Take the stairs to the second floor. At the second floor there will be a door labeled "2." Open the door. You'll want to turn left inside the hallway, and take another left. There's no other way to go, so you shouldn't have any trouble with this part! On the left-hand side of the hallway you'll see my apt., No. 265 (I know, I haven't changed the code to unlock the doors downstairs yet, and I should probably get around to that, but I knew you'd be looking after Sinamyn and this would make things easier, so I've been putting it off), about three doors down on the left. The floors here are all original hardwood, so if you're wearing heels, they tend to clack quite loudly. That's not a problem, unless you're coming at those really early or late times, because I wouldn't want you to wake up the neighbors. Mrs. Gitlen, (across the hall) is kind of old, and rather suspicious, and I don't think she sleeps much, or she is a terribly light sleeper, and she might wake up and think you're a stranger and call the police.

Once you're inside the apt. (the other day at work I gave you two keys. The round one's for the deadbolt, the square one's for the knob; I had them made that way so you wouldn't get them mixed up), the kitchen counter will be on your left, and that's where I usually set down my purse when I come home. It's just a convenient place to put down your things so that you can get settled before taking care of Sinamyn. By the way, thanks so much for this; you're a big help!

FEEDING:

Sinamyn only needs to eat once a day (she's been on a diet since she started puffing up, and the vet said that for her age she shouldn't be putting on that much weight, so I'm not feeding her as much).

To the right of the kitchen counter you'll find the refrigerator. On the right side of the refrigerator is the refrigerator compartment. The left side is the freezer. You shouldn't need to get into the freezer at all, especially if you don't give in to Sinamyn's whining for more food! I've left enough for her to cover the day I'm gone, but should you need any extra, there's some in the freezer. If you open the freezer, on the middle shelf (the bottom shelf contains my ice cream. Sorry, I know there's a lot of ice cream. I don't know why I'm saying sorry about that; it's my ice cream and I shouldn't feel bad; I'm just thinking what you might be thinking when you see all that ice cream. Well, you know what kind of month it's been, so you probably understand) you'll find Ziploc freezer bags of Sinamyn's food. These have been frozen to preserve the flavors, because I read online that if the food is kept in its packaging at room temperature for more than six months, it gets bland. I don't know how it is that they know that. Can you imagine? So, should you need more food take one freezer bag and set it in the big pot in cold water in the sink to defrost. That's how I do it. I don't like to use the microwave, because eventually—even on defrost—it starts to cook the food, and then it turns into this mushy mess that Sinamyn won't even look at. If you turn around from the refrigerator, you'll be facing the island that sits in the middle of the kitchen, where the sink is. To the left of the sink, and below it, is a cupboard, and inside you'll find pots and pans. The "Big Pot" I use, is the dutch oven-looking one that has the clear lid and sits on the bottom shelf of the cupboard. Just drop the freezer bag into the pot, cover it with water from the tap and let it sit in the sink. It usually takes about twenty minutes to defrost. Feel free to watch television while you're waiting. You can also watch TV while Sinamyn's eating, before you take her on her walk. If there's nothing good on the TV, I have every season of *Buffy* on DVD. Operating instructions for the television and DVD player follow below . . .

## PLAYING HANDS

He'd fallen in love with his hands. The fingers had once combed through the black tendrils milimetering out from a woman's head. They'd also graced the elastic waistband of his Jockeys, and the keys of a Casio electronic keyboard. He hadn't an ear for music, and disparate notes—a sound like the transmission of a machine that crushes the spent husks of what were once vehicles, which families had ripped around America—drifted out from the hands. The hands themselves had turned into mangroves. Every finger sprouted yet another finger and then another finger, and the hands were the mangrove root system for the canopy of his head. But it was beautiful still, he thought, the fact of his playing.

## PSYCHOGENIC POLYDIPSIC

This Freak can be found holding up bars whilst sitting atop his barstool. Or these may be horses confined to their pens without Nintendo, and so their boredom is intolerable. Either way the results are the same: the fluids consumed outweigh typical jello-filled bathtubs. And we mean old bathtubs, the kind with animal claws for feet. Worried of your own propensity toward beverages? Among questions to ask the psychogenic polydipsic: Have you been indulging in a profusion of burritos or Russian salads? Have you been skipping rope in the immediate vicinity of active volcanoes? Have you found yourself pissing down the length of telephone poles? In most cases, polydipsics are mathematicians in Hollywood films, and so you shouldn't worry. True psychogenic polydipsics suffer from middle-finger-out-the-window-of-their-Mercedes syndrome, and the left armpits of their undershirts are stained yellow. Just the same, keep an eye on your horse. Psychogenic polydipsics are people who are always fucking thirsty, forever, what I mean is, pass the wine.

## ROMANCE NOVEL, THE

In this literary genre the heroine is always a plucky young lawyer who has never had sex. She has spent all her years heretofore playing Scattergories. She is an excellent player of Scattergories. Ask her for an airline that starts with D, and she'll nail you with Delta. Same goes for letters of the Greek alphabet and sorority sisters, for military operations and platoons. She is, but of course, terribly lonely. It is terrible; it fills her with terror. And so she never watches movies, because of the dark. This, she knows, is among clichéd steps toward reconciling the loneliness, and yet she is somewhat thrilled by the terror. Yet another word that begins with L and aptly describes things is a label. The accountant in the office across from hers retrieves her mail and deposits it upon her desk each morning, like a retriever might belch a ball. Her retriever in fact does this every evening when our heroine slouches home, her hair exactly like a bird's nest down to the twine, bra of plastic, the pecking seagull fledglings. There is a break at this moment to unbearably go over the fortunes of all involved characters: the accountant's accounts, the lawyer's laws, all of their incomes, their prospects (bleak) and who would prefer to marry whom (equally bleak). This tirade keeps up for something like two hundred pages. Unlike the lawyer's retriever, the accountant is a human, and he stands in front of the plucky woman's desk not with a sad longing look for human attention, but with that carefully poised demeanor of a man who begs for affection. What we mean is, he has one hand on one hip. Our heroine, however, thinks the guy at the gym—the one in the Spandex—is way hot. This is the same formula as in the romantic comedy film, except it is a little bit funnier. In the end the aliens attack and instead of Spandex or receipts there are machines and explosions, a ripped skirt that exposes a soft but muscular feminine thigh, and Will Smith shows up for a bit, because—well, Christ, man, what's a movie without Will Smith? Never mind the movie. In the novel, the dramatic climax reaches its pinnacle mid-trial, when our lawyer-heroine is illogically unaware of the prosecution's surprise (also illogical) witness (because that doesn't happen in real life because that is a step in the legal process called Discovery) and she pulls the rug out from under everyone, and this sends judge, jury, witness, prosecution, innocent bystanders—everyone—sprawling with rug burn, and the judge holds our main character in contempt. Now no one finds her attractive at all, and she has been debarred. Oh, poop.

## RUSSIANS

In Russia there are so many Russians! It's like one of those neighborhoods where a bunch of Russians live, but way bigger. This place is big. It's like they took a country the size of Russia and filled it with Russians. One cannot slip through Mayakovskaya Station without listening in on a spit forth "Neeyet!" or "Spice-eeba!" which are the Russians' favorite words. These mean, respectively, *I will not smile for your photograph*, and *our cuisine is not very spicy*. Every Russian has a little piece of the world's largest country, and that piece is among the world's smallest apartments, except for the Japanese (see *Japanese, The* pg. 74). Should you—god forbid—go whistling Dixie in one of these microscopic rooms, every microscopic ruble and microscopic kopek sprouts microscopic wings and flaps away in a dizzying scatter of impoverished fractals. Every Russian also has a bear pedaling a too-small bicycle around their living room, a bear wielding a hockey stick. While the bicycle is fitting for this room's size, the bear is not. How this was accomplished is yet to be determined. All that's known is that for more than sixty years Russia has been an international leader in science and technology. In Russia there are no cold drinks in one of Earth's coldest countries. Want ice water? That'll be room temperature. Meantime ice floats down the Arbot, down Nevsky Prospekt, down all the streets, which are themselves rivers of ice. Want a cold beer? Room temperature beer is ubiquitous in Russia. In fact, all of the liquid in Russia is beer. Or tea. Even the Russian's blood—composed of beer and tea—is room temperature: thirty-seven degrees

Celsius. And good God, when you enter these rooms, stripping off your boots and fifty-two layers, the Russians start toasting you. They toast your health, your visit, your friends, your family, your pets. They toast toasting. Then they'll kiss your sweaty cheeks, and you'll learn the Cyrillic alphabet.

## SAN FRANCISCANS

San Franciscans are most noted for their dreadlocks. In fact, when seen by astronauts hovering in the blue glow of the thermosphere, San Francisco proves to be one enormous dreadlock. All of Earth's patchouli—a substance cultivated primarily in regions known for their human rights abominations—is exported to San Francisco. Thus, the air surrounding San Francisco, extending into the stratosphere, has had its trace elements replaced by patchouli and molecules of Dungeness crab. San Franciscans are fond of tacos and flat landscapes. Summers, one finds San Franciscans huddled around the hulking burning body of a wooden man, a wooden man in the shape of an inverse taco, placed in a distant desert, a desert flatter—even—than San Francisco. San Franciscans are Earth's most patient humans. Should you employ yourself in this vicinity, take it easy, don't worry about it, you'll get there when you get there. San Francisco is currently undergoing an immense digitization project. The goal: by 1999 San Franciscans will have reversed time and converted San Francisco, having contained it inside a Silicon Valley web server. There, all the San Franciscans will utter *San Francisco* into eternity. This is fortunate, since the west coast of San Francisco is a transverse fault, and soon San Francisco will become Alaska, and Alaskans have already stockpiled ammunition in preparation for this dreadlocked invasion. The Alaskans have done this under the auspices of wildlife sportsmanship, but the San Franciscans—thank God—will save them, and themselves. Perhaps they'll save all of us through their recycling program. We are all of us in desperate need of renewal.

SECOND TITLE PAGE

# The Book of Freaks

Jamie Iredell

## SHOE FOR A HEAD

The man with a shoe for a head told everyone to look for him in their local Athlete's Foot. He said, you should really buy my head. He said, go hard or go to the grocery store, and, just make your way through the world, you pussy, and, if I'm not in you then you don't have a man with a shoe for a head inside you and that's just a sad thing. He had a wife who had a tooth for a head. If you could have heard her, she would have said things like, you wouldn't believe all the things that get stuck between me. Their children were frogs, but not real frogs. They were the kind of frogs that look exactly like the puppet frogs on a children's television program. How the man with a shoe for a head, or his wife with a tooth for a head, or their puppety frog kids, or you, or the compilers of this volume, got to be the way we are is anyone's guess.

## SISTERS

almost always live tragic lives. They'll march with their brothers into fields polka-dotted with strawberries. The youngest—a towhead—will say his finger has found the furthest reaches of his nose, which tickles, and that the sky has turned pink. The middle one—Michelle, the sister we're speaking of, brace-toothed and bespectacled—will say, "Shut up, Bobby. You're such an *idiot*." The strawberry arched from her fingers in a parabola of streaked red will splatter Bobby's shirt so that it resembles a television gunshot wound. Jacob, the freckled chubby oldest, will fill the inside of his headlock with Michelle's curled locks. Another berry—smashed upon those curls—will resemble the brains that tick away under Michelle's scalp, the mind itself overcome with singular hatred. The middle child, a girl, the one they call "Four-eyes," and "Lispy," for her retainered Ss.

"You fat ass," Michelle will holler from within Jacob's elbow. It will sound like she is deep inside a cave, locked away, which, of course, she is. There are things these brothers will never know: the twisted ruined barn beyond the southern hills, the old man and his son, the hundreds of colored bottles, that to those men she is beautiful and wanted.

When Jacob releases her, the hills will sparkle not with strawberries and brothers, but with dew, alight with sunset, dappled like a tuxedo's white-rosed lapel, the scent of mango carried in from the sea.

## THICK HAIR

In such situations, for these humans, beneath her hair lay more hair, the black strands cables holding up the suspension bridge that is her head. If you could peer through these fibers—and few can—you would spy yet another world living upon her scalp. Her skull is the mantle of this planet, the skin a crust, the hair an atmosphere. Under this atmosphere, running about, tiny mothers in tiny minivans, with tiny bumper stickers with the wee-est messages scrawled across them: *I vote for level-headed-ness*. Let's forget the word "tiny," now that that's obvious. A mechanic has a tow truck. He is grease-splattered. His grease-splatteredness makes its way all across the globe. This is the man of our woman's dreams—our woman with the thick hair. What we—the compilers of this volume—mean, is that this man had once shaved his goatee and when he did so he entered the woman's dreams. He fell through her scalp-crust, fell through the thin fatty layer, fell through the parietal, into the cerebral cortex, and thus became a dream of a man with no goatee. When he emerged he was inextricably changed: he ordered a cleanup of the world of the woman's scalp. This mechanic's greasiness became biodiesel, the scalp area grew more atmospheric hair. The tiny—sorry—people of this tiny—sorry again—world, breathed wonderful air. The woman ended up on a television commercial where she flipped her hair through air lit by a director of photography's lights. This woman became famous even if only for a while. Then everyone forgot about her and her thick hair. And everyone upon her scalp died and the planet went extinct. And then the woman died the way all women die: her hands were crossed over her body peacefully.

## TINY HEAD

Yet another name for this condition is microcephalic. Said tiny headed enjoy watching YouTube clips of golfers crashing through windshields like golf balls. That is the funniest shit ever to the tiny headed, that people care about it is funnier still. What they should care about is Seinfeld jokes. Why do people eat ice cream, what they should do is not eat ice cream. What they should care about is people like this: a tiny head. Tiny head is what they always call those with tiny heads. Usually, their circus name is tiny head. They can be found riding a bicycle while a doctor measures their head. The fact that a tiny head can even ride a bicycle most say is a miracle, and tiny heads say fuck them they know nothing about what goes on in my tiny head. The fact that this is written—this too—about them, the synapses firing like the fires of stars in galaxies, and the web of galaxies floating in dark matter is just like the inside of their tiny head. The doctors do not realize that in the dark matter is where real thinking takes place because real thinking is not conscious it is a ramble like a mountain it is vast and full of life yet at the top of the tiny head there are not any trees because life finds it hard to take root at the top of mountains, so tiny head is bald and some people say they are bald as a baby's ass and tiny head thinks that's plain stupid don't you.

TITLE PAGE

# The Book of Freaks

## TOWN KIDS

Children from towns across North America, on BMXs, swig whisky-sworled Kool-Aid most afternoons shriek-dusted by autistics. South of the seagull shit-cracked porches the bricks and windows are August-wired open. Wails whip through cottonwoods, find the ends of Camel Wides, Black n' Sweet Backwoods, the tattered ear somebody's daddy shear-mangled with the kitchen chicken-splitters for stacking the canned peas and carrots like a list, like a stack of lists. The screams are the wails of seagulls, are the town's kids, that night their mothers hid the whisky. But—and good thing—they found it.

## TUMOR, THE

Celled its way to a golf ball-sized clump of cells. Tumors and certain weather phenomena are always compared to sporting balls and fruit. Example: *There's a grapefruit-sized tumor in his colon. Our town was pummeled by softball-sized hail.* Why are not tumors and hail tumor and hail-sized? The doctors and meteorologists wander their offices tapping pencils to their temples and eyeing through stacks of *Sports Illustrated*, their walls wallpapered with fruited still lifes. This particular tumored man, about whom we're discussing, possessed good teeth, bad gums. His gums smelled like dead flesh. He jogged. His heart was a very fat man's, and he pounded it inside his chest. As many syllables as "cardio vascular disease" lined by on a sign inside his head. His tumor was a basketball under his shirt. Sex evaporated as quickly as his wife's presence in his apartment. His body remained, tumor-attached. The body was named Larry. Outside the hail was the size of hail.

## UNITED ARAB EMIRATIANS

What most do not know about United Arab Emiratians is their prowess with the discus. Even the minutest of the Emiratians can hurl a discus, spinning and skimming moisture from the air, for more than a hundred meters. This was discovered—the cover removed and what was underneath shown to the rest of the world—in California, where there are few United Arab Emiratians. But those who migrated, came to the brink of American Olympic glory, only to be ousted for performance drug abuse. Next to the discus, United Arab Emiratians are adept club openers, managers, and bouncers. One can find these failed Olympic hopefuls admiring their slicked oil locks in the ever-present mirrors walling up these otherwise velveted interiors. Should you—man, you're an idiot if you do, but anyway—show up to an Emiratian's club female-less, then never mind your Friday night. No, no, my friend. There are twenty-four-hour diners where losers like you can dip French fries into your Heinz and taste yourself getting fatter. This is only because of the United Arab Emiratian's extreme appreciation for all things beautiful. The compilers of this volume have been in a taxi captained by one of these countrymen, a taxi that taxied past a glorious wreck. Forget the fact that the compilers were late for an important lecture on the merits of Chekhovian description techniques in fiction. This cab driver slowed to a halt, admiring the twisted and shining chrome, dripping with the drizzle raining down. The last sputter of exhaust and steam from the overturned undercarriage. The bright splash of red from the crying woman's sweatshirt. This Emiratian could have been admiring the engineering feat and beauty of his home country's mastery with the skyscraper, their towers much higher than any mountain in the United Arab Emirates, or their ability to adopt capitalism, their tireless lust for improvement. "My God," said the Emiratian, "look at *that*."

## VAMPIRE, A

This particular vampire was observed upon a spear of summer grass, and again in a local taquería. A volume of something stupid sweats in the sweat of his fingers, reading "a novel" on its cover. If you breathe garlic breath at this vampire's pores, nothing happens. He is large, he contains multitudes. Buy him a Silver Bullet, and he'll gag. Remember: this man said "vampire," not "werewolf," and that only frat boys like Coors Light. This is the truth that dangles from every crucifix. This man says that Jesus is quite beautiful. He sweats holy water; his body sings the electric. The bar splinter, driven into his chest by leaning for the Jameson, does nothing. He is all: bodies, souls, air, earth, exclamations, promulgations, the dead, the living, the handmaid carrying her wares, the workman hefting his, the poet with his poems, the poems with their poems, the poems' poems within their own little universes contain all and everything of this, the vampire sings. He says, "If I bite you, will you become me?" You should at this point be thinking, "Hopefully."

## VERY FAT

This is the medical term for severely overweight individuals. One particular man weighed in at 1,264 pounds, and even the scale—which was digital, and set into the floor beneath the steel bed frame—read "Holy shit!" He had not always been so large. He hardly breathed, for all the eating. If food itself contained oxygen, that was his air. Remember your mother telling you not to eat watermelon seeds for what would eventually grow inside you? He never left his bed. In order to be fed and cleaned, he had a girlfriend who'd shed tears when they met. She was the kind of woman who would clean up after men who slapped her behind and called her "shugah," and she'd never stopped smiling. She wanted him to lose weight. But the bacon he sucked up satisfied her, also the grease he dabbed at with his bread crust. These two are still together, though the prognosis is bleak.

## VITAMIN D DEFICIENCY

This condition results from leaving for work in darkness and returning home after sundown. Work is as an accountant. All members in this firm firmly believe in eventually being in the black. Sufferers dream dreams of a dairy farm, of becoming a cheese maker. They and their boyfriends have begun making cheese in their tiny Seattle apartment on weekends. This, they say, is a very involved process, so they cannot get outside. Even if they did, the sky is covered by clouds that drizzle mist. In the world there are novelists who tell these accountants that they are cheese making vampires, them and their boyfriends—all men such novelists have never met—and that they'll make novels about them and collect billions of dollars. The accountant-cheese makers say their goat cheese is pretty good but not the right texture, though they're working on that. None of the boyfriends have the name of Patrick.

## WE

Only *watch* baseball these days.

## WHAT WE CALL LIFE

In life people stand on beaches under white clouds. They all stare at the clouds, though there's nothing about the clouds that makes a discernable shape or could be in any way interesting. Some say that this was before language, but those making this distinction assume a false sense of superiority, which is almost always rousted out by way of their automobile choices and style of dress. This is universally true of domestically-produced autos and imported clothing. What is perhaps most notable, however, is viewing subjects in the convenience store. There aren't any beaches in this state. But if there were, even these people would stand around like those staring at clouds, unsure of what beer to choose.

## WHITE PEOPLE

While goofing around on YouTube the other day we came across a video of Mitch Hedberg who said that non-racists love all people: white people, black people, green people, purple people. He said we've got to draw the line somewhere: fuck purple people, unless they are suffocating, then help them. It would've been good if that joke had been ours. But seriously, white people are fucking crazy. They have flags and leather pants and boots and can be most proficient with profanities and stones. They seem perpetually bound to the television screen, upon which they are found rallying, their signs etching political statements in the sky: I disagree with you! White people eat funny foods: this stuff called Tex-Mex, and then there's chowder. Why would anyone call foodstuff chowder? Better to have named it candy surprise. White people always have jobs, but never work. Somehow, though, they keep the Earth in rotation, likely with a billion purple people pedaling stationary bicycles. Meantime, yet another billion green people yank an enormous rope and tug (à la o'-war) the planet round the sun, the force of these poor souls' exertions the cause of said planet's characteristic wobble. White people live in Vermont, where they attend writers' conferences and exclaim, "Ahhh! Fall color!" To be a true non-racist one must concede: fuck white people.

## WIVES

fulfill an important role in most societies by telling their husbands that they are babies.

## WRITING ON THE WALL, THE

It tilts along, a feminine hand. Every *e* curls like a tongue, the word *tongue*, in fact, tastes the wall. The wall tastes the girl's hand. The hand, sweat-salted from wheelchair-pushing, grease-grimed from bridging glasses to her nose's bridge (that part of her nose was flat, just like a bridge, which makes this cliché an apt metaphor) was a road to her mind. Her eyes were holes that sucked in the world's light, the light mother-darkened by a mother with a voice as rough as the wall.

## YERBA BUENIANS

Yerba Buenians are an extinct race that met disaster after filling in the primary cove upon which their modest settlement was initially built with their mostly unused names. *Yerba Buena* refers to the Anglicization of the original settlement's native name of *Hierva Buena Que Rica en la Boca de Las Mujeras Bellisimas de España Vieja*; however, the original meaning of this name has been lost to history, much like the Yerba Buenians themselves. Yerba Buenians were known as a wild and rambunctious tribe, having strung numerous of their settlement's highest officials by their necks from the edifices of the administrative and religious centers. For example, their founder, José Joaquín de la Santísima Trinidad Moraga, and the party's original leader, Juan Bautista de Anza Bezerra Nieto, were usurped by the insurrectionist Juan Ramirez Tuaca Guadalupita de Rosa de Santa María de la Revolución de Los Angeles del Rio de la Amazonianos con la Leche Sabrosa y Dulce y la Café Muy Dudo. Other Yerba Buenians, such as Rosa Miguelita Carmela de la Ascención de la Vírgen de Guadalupe que Regresa del Corazon de Tu Madre Quando Ella Tiene la Cochinita Sucia y Lavale en El Rio Pequeño, enjoyed their purchased salmon from Vancouverians who had established trade relations prior to the country's disappearance. At the height of a large migratory invasion of Americans, the Yerba Buenians' population skyrocketed, causing the phone book to expand exponentially by the length of its pages, thus Yerba Buena Cove was filled with a billion seemingly unnecessary names. As a result, Yerba Buenian culture fizzled and sputtered in collusion with their new migratory neighbors, and was subsumed completely by the time the town and its inhabitants' names were changed. They became San Franciscans (see *San Franciscans*, pg. 105).

## ZIMBABWEANS

It has been well documented that Doris Lessing is a big fan of Zimbabweans, and that the cultural, political, and geographic details of these people and their region have filled her works with pizzazz. In fact, it is safe to refer to Lessing's work as *stylized*. Even William Zinser has proclaimed to be a devout follower of Lessing's writings. They are good writings. They are Lessing's writings. In just one of Lessing's writings the Zimbabweans are treated ever so harshly under the stark racial divide—driven like a constant zephyr across the sub-Saharan plains—between the natives and their Anglo-colonial overseers. But, never mind Lessing, let us get to the actual Zimbabweans. Zimbabweans are a generous and intelligent people with an intricate culture that has existed since what an American college freshman would call "the dawn of time." By this, said college freshman means, since the beginning of human history, since humans are the organisms that invented the concept of time, as well as metaphors for describing such abstract phenomena, such as "dawn." Ancient Zimbabweans were adept architects of ziggurats. Like above-mentioned college freshmen, whose concepts of closure often involve the walking into metaphorical depictions of our planet's rotation in its infinite journeying round our star, Zimbabweans will be found walking as silhouette into sunset.

## ZE-END

Ze-end (zē ĕnd): an efficient Teutonic buzz replaces the effete *th* of the English; otherwise the pronunciation is much the same. To pronounce it with the proper authority one must smoke a cigarette at the same time, holding it in the peculiar underhand fashion of pre-1945 Germany—or pre-1989 East Germany—as if a needle to be precisely inserted into a vein, and not casually hooking it between the index and middle knuckles à la Humphrey Bogart. Ideally, black should also be worn along with highly polished thigh-high leather boots. The monocle is optional. "The end" (thē ĕnd), without an accent, when announcing the conclusion of a story, but more commonly (thə ĕnd) with the schwa e so faintly pronounced, the two words frequently elide (thĕnd), the speaker typically having been so fatigued by the misguided euphoria of the beginning and the long complex confusion of the middle to expend any effort on the extra syllable. Songs with this title never make sense. Those who pen the lyrics to such songs are more appropriately posted on the posters of teenage girls' bed and dorm rooms. The idea of an end precludes that of a beginning. The universe defies this supposition. As we have learned, the beginning was a donut. The end, therefore, is spaghetti. Westerns of that variety, anyhow: windswept plains and rolling tumbleweeds, a be-holstered thigh and cowboy-capped noggin, scraggly cheeks. It is noon, and the sun is high, so we shall say high noon. An American saunters along the wooden sidewalk. Click clack goes a bullet chambered. Wait, maybe the end is a kiss, lips parted drawing near, the outline of bodies making even a heart silhouette in the beach sunset. Back it up and the men part yet again, distance themselves from one the other, a wave of goodbye. Perhaps the end contains explosions (see *Action Film, The* pg. 2), the space cruiser scuttling away with a roar of inexplicable engines somehow captured from the reader's (viewer's?) point of view in space's vacuum. The explosion, likewise a tremendous candle snuffing, a sneeze, an ejaculation, molecules and dust spread only to coalesce with gravity over what the documentary narrators call millennia, though it's more like billenia, and yet another star will burst forth. In the end, the heroine survives the slasher's onslaught, knives dripping and ripping air, gunfire, rollers rolling their lights across suburban house frames, sirens like sirens of a Greek epic lulling the stupefied to what seems to spell safety. But the whale will ram the whaler, the lovers' forebemoanéd moan silenced with a poisoned kiss, but that slow-boy-grown-to-a-slow-man-child's rage bellows from the carriage round Jefferson's Confederate monument, and don't you know that god is pooh bear? And the end should've ended just after we said all right then we'll go to hell. Or when that bullet passed through Lenny's cerebral cortex; when Rosasharn offers her stillborn's milk to the starving, when the flood waters recede; when they nailed up the man who invented the church; when the great rich guy floats in his estate's own pool; when the dueling swords end their play and make amends before poison overtakes and Norway invades; when the dragon's dead like the aging hero; when those who were not the one dead turned to their affairs; when Anna throws herself under the train; when, like a Zimbabwean, we saunter off, sunset-bound.

# Other Books from Future Tense

Ventriloquism *by Prathna Lor, $5*

OK, Goodnight *by Emily Kendal Frey and Zachary Schomburg, $5*

Put Your Head in My Lap *by Claudia Smith, $5*

Everything Was Fine Until Whatever *by Chelsea Martin, $11*

Embrace Your Insignificance: Lessons Learned Teaching English in Japan *by Bob Gaulke, $11*

Our Beloved 26th *by Riley Michael Parker, $3*

Partial List of People to Bleach *by Gary Lutz, $6*

Dahlia Season: Stories and a Novella *by Myriam Gurba, $15*

Before You She Was a Pit Bull *by Elizabeth Ellen, $5*

*Future Tense Books*

www.futuretensebooks.com

Breinigsville, PA USA
29 March 2011
258625BV00001B/6/P